PRAISE FOR SHEEP AND WOLVES

"Stripped down to the bare bones of narrative consciousness, these stories manipulate the reader like a drunken Trix Rabbit buggering the corpse of Kurt Vonnegut."
—Cameron Pierce, author of *Shark Hunting in Paradise Garden*

"The stories contained in Sheep and Wolves are like a series of car accidents. You know you shouldn't be looking, but you can't take your eyes off the pages stained with blood and fingers and all the horror and madness."
—*The Orange Spotlight*

"I've put this book down, but it's one that I pick up at least once a week and flip to a random section and read that story again. There is no question that Jeremy Shipp has captured lightning in a bottle here."
—*ZombieMall*

"*Sheep and Wolves* does not believe in beach reading or in hammocks and hot chocolate. It does not believe in love at first sight or in happy marriages....Welcome to the bizarro fiction movement; hail Jeremy C. Shipp."
—*Oxyfication*

"Better than Pynchon's *Gravity's Rainbow*."
—Scott Lefebvre, author of *Spooky Creepy Long Island*

Acknowledgements

"Camp" first published in *ChiZine*
"Baby Edward" first published in *Greatest Uncommon Denominator*
"Nightmare Man" first published in *Hub*
"Watching" first published in *Bare Bone*
"American Sheep" first published in *Star-Spangled Zombie*
"The Hole" first published in *The Swallow's Tail*
"Those Below" first published in *Love & Sacrifice*
"Scratch" first published in *Bust Down the Door and Eat All the Chickens*
"Flapjack" first published in *The Bizarro Starter Kit (blue)*

Published by Raw Dog Screaming Press
Hyattsville, MD

First Edition

Cover design: Jennifer C. Barnes
Book design: M. Garrow Bourke

Printed in the United States of America

ISBN: 978-1-933293-52-3 / 978-1-933293-59-2

Library of Congress Control Number: 2008935330

www.rawdogscreaming.com

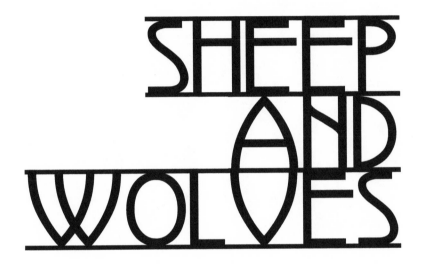

SHEEP AND WOLVES

COLLECTED FICTION

JEREMY C. SHIPP

**RAW DOG
SCREAMING
PRESS**

For those I love.

And for those creatures on this planet who deserve so much more respect than they ever receive.

CONTENTS

WATCHING

YOU DON'T HAVE to enjoy watching while Gerald masturbates onto his first cousin, or Nadine carefully chokes herself with an antique bonnet, or Carter craps into an urn that he stores under the kitchen sink. You just have to pretend. You have to sit back, sniff the cinnamon stick that you keep hidden in your glove, and give them what they want.

"What's the knife for, Felix?" I say.

He paces back and forth, and I try to focus on the sound of his boots smacking the wooden floor, instead of the blood dribbling down his chin and the bite marks covering his arms.

"I'm not going to hurt you," Felix says. "You know I'm gentle as a fly."

"You mean you wouldn't hurt a fly," I say.

"Whatever. I'll pay you two thousand if you watch me do this." He puts his hand on top of his dresser, next to a brick. "I won't pass out. I'll drive myself to the hospital. Seriously. Please."

"You know I can't," I say. "Janette would fire me if she knew—"

"Don't tell her. We'll keep this between you and me."

"It doesn't work that way."

"We'll make it work."

"I can't."

"You know what you are, Sebastian?" He points the knife at my face. "You're a fucking tease!"

This isn't supposed to happen. I sniff my glove.

Felix glances at his weapon and says, "Sorry." He lowers the knife so fast, he loses his grip. I'm afraid the blade will bounce against the floor and find its way to my face or heart, but it doesn't. It only lays there.

"I would never hurt anybody," Felix says. "You know that."

"I know," I say. I pretend.

He kneels and cradles the knife in both hands. He looks like he might start crying. "You think I'm disgusting."

"No, Felix," I say. "If it were up to me, I'd stay here and watch. I want to see you do it. Really."

He grins.

And so do I.

Janette searches my face, and I try to focus on the statues standing on the shelf behind her. There's the Amazon with her missing right breast. Janette once told me that these mythological women sometimes cut off their breasts so they could improve their bow shooting. She also told me that the Ancient Greeks believed that women needed to be tamed by their fathers and husbands, otherwise they would all be wild whores. She said that it's this sort of taming that brings new working girls to her doorstep year after year.

"Felix showed up at the ER an hour after your session ended," Janette says. "With a missing finger."

"Damn it," I say. I'm impressed that Janette procured this information so quickly, but not surprised. She has contacts everywhere, most willing to spill their guts for a discount. "I can't believe he really did it."

She stares at me for a while longer.

Next to the Amazon rests the Siren, with her angel wings and her duck feet. The Ancient Greeks believed that men and men alone had the power to tame their sexual urges. Only they could protect their families from the siren-like powers of other women.

"I reviewed your session with Felix," Janette says, and taps the digital voice recorder on her desk. "You both are excellent actors."

"I wasn't acting," I say.

"When Felix gets upset, he stumbles with his words, and he wasn't stumbling. Everything else was believable enough though. Good job."

"It wasn't an act, Janette."

"The fact that you kept a substantial payoff from me hurts, but I don't really care about the money. What really upsets me is that you're willing to endanger my entire operation for a few extra bucks. I test your blood and I know you're not a drug addict, Sebastian. What do you need the cash for?"

I search the room for answers, but there aren't any. "Nothing."

This time she looks at me like she's sorry for me.

Beside the Siren there's Baubo, with breasts for eyes and a vulva for a mouth. She once cheered up a goddess by flashing her. Janette told me that this wasn't a sexual thing. Baubo revealed the power of fertility that exists in all women. The Ancient Greeks believed that women were dirty inside and could pollute the world around them by menstruating and giving birth. Baubo didn't keep her power hidden, so the Ancient Greeks made her into a mutant.

"Did you eat it?" Janette asks.

"What?" I say.

"His finger."

"Of course not. Who do you think I am?" I stop looking past her, and meet her gaze.

"I believe you," she says. "The problem is that I'm not narcissistic enough to assume I can't be tricked. I need to make sure I know what you're capable of."

"What do you want me to do?"

"First of all, let me smell your breath."

I stand and lean over and breathe onto her face.

"I don't smell vomit," she says. "Or anything that might be used to cover up the smell of vomit. If you did eat it, it's still inside you."

"I watched him cut it off. I didn't eat it."

"It's only been a few hours, so you'd probably still have some finger in your stomach." She reaches under her desk and brings up a bucket, which she hands to me. "I'm going to need you to throw up. Then I'll send it off to the lab, and see if you're telling me the truth."

"I don't think I can vomit on command."

"Stick your finger down your throat."

"I tried that once and it didn't work."

She pulls a bottle of ipecac out of her drawer, just like I knew she would.

Soon I heave so hard I'm afraid my eyes will pop out, but they don't.

"Now go dump that in the toilet," she says.

"I thought you wanted to test it."

"I've tested you enough."

When I return with the bucket, she says, "I know I said I don't care about the money, but you're going to give me five thousand for this betrayal and the others I never found out about."

I only made three thousand from Felix. Still, this is fair. I nod to her.

She hands me a piece of orange paper with 'Valerie Trum' written on the top. "You have an all-nighter. Tonight at seven."

"I can't work tonight," I say. "I have a date."

"You have a date with Valerie Trum."

Janette may seem like a level-headed businesswoman, but she's actually a human being. Underneath her pinstriped suit there are scars on her wrists. She showed them to me during my first job interview with her, and scrutinized my reaction.

Now she's giving me that same look.

She's waiting.

"I shouldn't have betrayed you," I say. "I'm sorry."

She smiles a little. "Tonight at seven."

I turn on the voice recorder and say, "I hope you're happy," before knocking on the door of Valerie Trum's two-story cookie-cutter house. I'm not surprised she lives here. This place may look the same as every other home around, with only slits of yard between them, but that doesn't mean

I'm not going to enter a new world and see things I've never imagined.

What does surprise me is the smile I'm greeted with. The warmth.

"Sebastian," she says, and holds out her hand.

I shake.

"I like your gloves," she says. "They look homemade."

"They are," I say, holding them out for some reason.

"I'm guessing you're a cold person. Not...cold-hearted. I mean you feel cold easily. My girlfriend was a hot person. Before she died."

That's why I'm here, I'm guessing. Grief.

"It tends to get cold in here at night," she says. "Feel free to turn up the heat. The thermostat's over there in the hall."

"I'm sorry about your girlfriend," I say.

"Thanks. I'll show you where I want you."

So I follow her into a bedroom upstairs. A guestroom, by the looks of it. The only thing that really catches my eye is a quilt-covered column in the corner.

"Sit there," she says, pointing.

I sit on the comfy-looking chair facing the column. It is comfy.

"There's leftover pizza in the fridge if you get hungry," she says. "You can take off the pepperoni if you're a vegetarian. Or Jewish. Or don't like pepperoni."

"Thanks."

She walks over to the column, and slides off the quilt. She reveals an antique iron birdcage. Or maybe it's not an antique. Maybe it's just old.

An ugly orange bird sits on the perch in the cage. No, that's a doll. A rag doll.

What Valerie's going to do with this cage and doll, or to this cage and doll, I don't know, but I'm prepared.

I sniff my glove. Vanilla.

"Whenever you're ready," I say.

She smiles at me. "I'm going to sleep at my cousin's for the night. I'll be back in the morning to pay you."

I almost give her a funny look, but stop myself. Instead, I nod. "What is it you want me to do exactly?"

"Watch the doll."

"Am I looking for something specific?"

"I can't tell you. Well, I could, but I don't want to. I don't want to influence what you see by telling you anything beforehand. Anyway, if you want to drink something besides water, there's orange juice in the fridge. There might be some apple juice left."

"Thank you."

She shakes my hand again, and leaves.

Time doesn't really fly when you're stuck babysitting an inanimate object, but things could be worse. You could lack an imagination or have ADD. You could be one of those people who finds himself haunted by his demons when faced with solitude.

I'm lucky.

I could try to sneak out and manipulate the audio recording, but Janette would find out. Plus, anytime I look away from the doll for too long, I feel guilty.

Better to just make the best of a ridiculous situation.

It's eight o'clock, and Snow's off work. I'll call her.

"I'm not going to be able to make it tonight," I say. "I got called into work."

"Shit," she says. "When does it start?"

"I'm here right now actually. It's OK that I'm talking with you though. My client's gone."

"Why's he gone?"

"She. It doesn't really matter. I'd invite you over, but it's against the rules."

"I know."

"I know you know. I wanted to say it anyway."

"Thank you."

"Can we have a phone date instead?"

"Yeah. Let me drive home first. I don't have one of those handless phone sets and I don't want to drive with one hand in the crap-mobile."

We say goodbye, and I'm alone with the doll again.

My heart beats fast and I don't feel cold at all. Even after all this time, Snow still makes me feel nervous and excited.

The first time I met Snow, the nervousness I felt wasn't so heavenly. She was one of my first clients, and I remember the way she touched my arm, comforting me. Even though I was there to comfort her.

She told me how thankful she was that her parents hadn't mutilated her body as a baby. But she was afraid. She hadn't told any of her friends that she was an intersexual. And she'd never shown her naked adult body to anyone but her doctor.

Then she showed me.

I didn't have to look past her large clitoris and pretend that she was beautiful. She was. Is. Mind, body, heart and soul.

I glance at my wrist, but I left my watch at home. No matter. Fifteen minutes until she calls. In the meantime, I can entertain myself by clicking my teeth together in time to the music in my head.

Click click click...

Click click click...

I hate this song.

Click click click...

The doll lifts her arm. Slowly, trembling.

Instantly, I know that Valerie Trum is a cruel woman who's trying to scare me.

Instantly, I'm clutching the chair, holding my breath.

The doll waves at me.

One of my hands relaxes, as if I'm going to release the arm rest and wave back. I sniff my glove instead.

The moment her arm drops, I stand. I try to focus on the chill slithering up and down my neck, but it's not enough.

I step forward and don't see any strings.

I reach inside the cage through the bars, because I don't have the key to the lock on the door.

She has to be mechanized. I need to touch her to find out.

I wrap my gloved hand around her and squeeze.

Nothing but fluff.

When I release her, she falls off the perch. I'm afraid she's going to jump back up and lunge for my face, but she only lays there.

I scream a little when the phone rings.

We greet each other with the usual routine, then move on.

"So you're just sitting around staring at the wall?" Snow says, laughing.

I wince. "Not exactly. Snow, I'm not...doing very well right now."

"What do you mean?"

"I mean...I think I'm losing it. My mind, I guess."

"Do you want to tell me about it?"

I shake my head, though I know she can't see that.

Snow reveals everything. My clients reveal everything. But me, I like to hide. It's a good thing Snow doesn't hate cowards.

"I don't think you're losing your mind," she says. "I think you're starting to deal with something that you haven't dealt with yet."

She's right. Before I can stop them, the words claw their way out of me. "I watched my client eat his own finger."

Silence. Then, "Why did you do that?"

"Because he paid me to."

She's silent again, and I can't hear anything else. "You have more than enough money," she says. "There's another reason."

I search the room. I even search the doll's black button eyes. Nothing.

"Jesus, Sebastian. Are you really such a stranger to yourself? You watched him eat his finger because you're a caring person. You didn't want him to feel ashamed anymore."

"I don't think that's true. I don't care about my clients. You're the only one—"

"You care."

I don't say anything for way too long.

"Call me back when you're ready to talk again," she says.

We end the conversation with the usual routine, then move on.

For me, that means watching the doll until I'm convinced that I didn't see what I saw.

I hear footsteps. Valerie Trum must be back to see how shook up I am because of her little trick. She'll probably laugh. She might even explain to me how she did it if I smile enough.

But no, the young woman who enters isn't Valerie Trum.

She sits on the floor, holding a bottle in her hands. She looks like she might start crying.

"Hello?" I say. "I'm a friend of Valerie."

She unscrews the top, and dumps a heap of blue pills onto the floor.

Now she does start crying.

No, that's not her.

The sound's coming from under the bed.

I step closer to the young woman. "Are you alright?"

A head slides out from under the bed and the crying consumes the room. Her body continues to wriggle across the floor until she's lying right beside me. The middle-aged woman runs a razor blade down the middle of her face.

The young sitting woman swallows the pills, handful after handful.

"Stop!" I say.

Watching isn't enough. I need to do something.

I reach down to grab the young woman's arm, and then I'm remembering a pink bedroom and a man named Uncle Daniel and—

I race for the door. It closes. Fast.

As soon as I turn around, another woman vomits on the floor right by my feet. I step over the mess, and face the wall. The orange sheet of paper in my pocket soon gives me Valerie Trum's cell phone number, and I call.

"What's going on here?" I say.

"You don't have to talk so loud," she says.

"What's going on here, Valerie?" I say, even louder.

"I honestly don't know," she says. "All I know is that she wanted a man. I hope you survive. You seem like a nice enough guy." With that, she hangs up. By the time I think of calling Snow, I've already thrown my phone against the wall and broken the damn thing in two.

The room roars with the chaos of women squirming, struggling, crying.

They're everywhere.

Cutting themselves, killing themselves.

Again and again and again.

The window slips open, and a flock of magazines fly inside. They cover the floor. They cover the walls. Maybe the ceiling, but I don't look up. They show me models and actresses and they're all screaming, tearing at their pages with bloody fingers. Trapped.

The women in the room don't stop suffering. No matter the fierceness of my commands. No matter how much they die.

Every time one of them passes through me, I feel them inside. Mind, body, heart and soul. I scramble around, jumping and spinning, trying to keep from being touched. From being violated. But it doesn't do any good.

I remember.

I remember the animals I saw in the popcorn ceiling above my bed and wishing that they would come alive and save me or eat me, and I remember how it felt when he ravaged my hymen and called me his sweet princess, and I remember the agony I felt every time my husband used me because they circumcised me as a baby, and I remember more and more until I collapse.

Everyone bends and funnels into the bird cage.

Silence again.

I try to stand, and by the third try I get to my feet.

I approach the cage.

The rag doll's standing on the perch, arms at her sides. She's trembling, and I'm sure this has nothing to do with weakness.

She's giving me that look.

She's waiting.

"I'm sorry," I say.

She shudders even more. Obviously she's not looking for an apology.

I consider walking away right now and spending the rest of my life trying to forget this ever happened. But the truth is, Snow was right. I do care about my clients.

This world, this system we live in, it doesn't treat my clients very well, and watching isn't enough.

Even after what this doll put me through, I don't know what it's like to be a woman. She does. She's charged with the energy of pain that I see oozing out my clients every day, in their blood, their semen, their shit.

The doll's charged up, and I think she's willing to do something about it.

If she's going to assassinate those who abuse power or lead a peaceful revolution, I don't know. It doesn't really matter. She can't sit back and watch these tragedies go on anymore. Anyway, the lock's already disappeared.

I open the cage.

NIGHTMARE MAN

THEY CALL IT postdormital paralysis with hypnopompic hallucinations.

I call it hell.

You open your eyes, and you think you're awake. But the room wheezes. A chthonic force seizes you, squeezing your chest, while a stark sonorous voice says, "You are doomed."

You are doomed.

Fear splatters against your skin and wiggles deep inside your gaping pores. Go ahead, toss and turn. Scream all you want. Until the presence absconds from your room, you're helpless. No one's going to save you.

The clock on the wall may say only 30 seconds have passed, but you know better.

Some moments last an eternity.

When this one ends, I'm free again. Free of the presence at least. I feel so much better than I did only seconds before, I should be celebrating. Dancing for joy.

Instead, I pop another pill. And another. This is my pathetic attempt at revenge.

"Take that," I think.

But deep down, I know he's laughing at me. He's saying, "You think you can harrow hell? I'll be back tomorrow."

He will.

Years ago, he only came once every few months. Then every few weeks. Days. Now, a night doesn't go by without an assault.

Yeah, I hate it. I hate him. But don't get me wrong. If the medication actually worked, I'd have never stopped taking it.

There are so many ways.

Sex, drugs, food.

Work, relationships, TV.

Talking, bathing, drawing the curtains and looking out the window.

When people say, "Get a life," what they usually mean is, "Drown out the screaming of your heart like I do, then we can be friends."

I refuse.

So I'm in my room, lying on my cot with my arms at my sides. Shapes coalesce in the popcorn ceiling. The trick isn't to stop seeing them. It's to ignore them without looking away.

My phone rings. For the first time in a very long while.

Sure, I could have disconnected the line years ago, but knowing that I'm not receiving any calls is just as important as the silence itself.

"Hello?" I say, barely.

"Tomas," he says. "It's Nabelung."

"Nabe," I say, and a hunk of slime leaps out of my throat onto my bare leg. It oozes toward my sheets.

"I'm sorry we haven't kept in touch, Tomas. You were always a good friend."

"No I wasn't."

He laughs a little, though I'm sure he knows I'm not joking. Then his voice gets serious. "Richard gave me your number. He told me what happened. I'm sorry."

"Thank you," I say, and barely mean it.

He's silent for a while. "This is going to sound strange. Well...it is strange. I know that. Especially coming from me. I was always such a skeptic."

"I never thought of you that way." My deep-seated spittle gently touches the fabric. "You believe in God."

"Yes, but in a regimented sort of way. That's not the point here, Tomas. I have a message for you. From a woman named Jade. She's been trying to contact you, but she can't get through."

The thought of a mysterious woman thinking about me makes me want to vomit. And her name, it almost brings me to tears. "I don't know anyone named Jade."

"You don't know her. She knows you. She says she wants you as her...well...she uses the word servant. I don't like the connotations of that word."

"What?"

"She told me if I didn't act as your invitation, she'd never stop bothering me. I'm sorry."

"Don't apologize."

"She says in order to see her, you need to eat a peanut."

"Salted or unsalted?" This is more of a knee-jerk reaction than anything. I used to joke around about everything, before I had nothing.

"She didn't specify that," he says. "But it has to look like a human face. Someone you know. She says you'll know it when you see it."

We're both silent for a while, he and I. It's very loud.

"That's about all I know," he says. "You can do with this what you want. I've done my part, so it's over for me now. Thank you for listening."

"Yeah."

"It was good speaking with you again, Tomas. I hope everything works out for the best. Goodbye."

He hangs up before I have the chance to speak. Before I can say something that I'll regret. He does this out of courtesy to me.

"Goodbye," I say.

They call them peanuts.

I call them indehiscent legumes that can fix atmospheric nitrogen and reduce the risk of heart disease.

Vitamin E, fiber, protein.

Monounsaturated and polyunsaturated fat.

Zinc, niacin, thiamin, manganese, folic acid, copper, phosphorous.

It used to be my job to know all this.

Now, the information buzzes in my mind and I swat it away. Unsalted peanuts are a part of my daily dinner plan. This one looks a little like standup comic Jim Gaffigan. He was one of my favorites back when I watched television and went to comedy clubs and combed my hair.

Years ago, I would have laughed. I would have shown it around like a trophy or a scar.

Now, I eat it. I crunch the miracle a few times, then swallow. Not because I want to see Jade. But because I refuse to believe in the power of a single peanut.

The old me would have believed. Or at least he would've wanted to. The old me believed that flax seed could cure cancer and that AIDS wasn't caused by a virus. He slid pamphlets under the doorways of unsuspecting strangers. He even hosted parties where he helped people to bend spoons with the power of their mind.

This was me.

Now he's gone.

The smiling peanut face is nothing but an acid-drenched memory.

Marshmallow peeps squirm in a massive cocoon-shaped heap on the tile floor. They move like desperate fingers, and I may be wrong about this, but I think some of them are. Little fingers. At first I don't know what the hell I'm doing here. Then I see the cats.

Oh, they're beyond hungry. They're dead, and they're out for blood. Piebald patches of black and white fur cling to their decaying flesh. I know they used to be good, sweet kittens who only tortured insects because they had no awareness of the bug's pain. But now, now they're in the know. They're pissed off at humanity because they would've loved us forever if we just hadn't thrown them away.

They charge not at me, but at the marshmallow cocoon. They know what it means to me even before I do.

"Stay away from them!" I say.

I kick the cats, one after another after another. They tumble on the floor and leave a trail of blood and fur and flesh in their wake. There are too many of them, and I'm not hindering the ones I'm punting away.

Soon, they're everywhere. They scratch and bite at the cocoon. Geysers of green blood spray out of the marshmallow chickens. I attempt to plug the holes with my fingers and toes, like some cartoon character trying to save a sinking ship. The cats, meanwhile, are purring like crazy. But whatever makes them purr is broken now. Now the purring sounds like a bean in a tin can being shaken by someone without any rhythm. There are a thousand beans and a thousand cans. I can taste the green blood in my mouth. More than that, I can taste the peanut.

The chickens and cats and carnage disappear to wherever they came from, and I'm alone.

I'm dreaming and I'm alone in a plain white room. More alone than I've ever been.

Oh, I'm beyond terrified.

I wish for the nightmare to return.

I even wish for the presence.

Instead, flecks of green light flitter in through cracks in the wall that I didn't notice before, and rally together into a blurry woman. She lacks details, but I can see that her hair is green and she's wearing a red dress. I think of Christmas for a moment. Then I don't.

"Tomas," she says.

After my name is spoken, I'm no longer looking down on the scene. I'm looking at the woman like I'm seeing with eyes. She's not only detailed, but exceedingly so. Every strand of her hair blares at me, the same as the cracks on the wall, and the intricate flower designs on the tile floor. I see these things like I'm staring inches from each of them, studying them with all my might. But I'm not.

"I'm Jade," she says. "But you already knew that."

She's right.

After sitting cross-legged, she pats the floor in front of her.

I take a step forward, though I don't sit down.

"You're afraid of me," she says. "Good. I'm glad you're not stupid."

"Yes I am," I say, almost rebelliously. Now I know I'm in trouble. The only time I talk back like this is when I'm feeling threatened beyond my ability to cope.

She waves away the thought. "You have no idea how hard it was to get in here. I was even considering contacting you in the waking time, but that never works. And when I say never, I mean it. No one's ever been open-minded enough to really hear me in the daylight. It's good that we can speak here. I'll have to thank Nabelung with some wonderful nightmares. The peanut worked."

"You're telling me this is happening because of some magical peanut?"

"In a sense. I know that human beings see human faces in anything and everything. All I had to do was get the idea planted in your mind by someone you respect. You did the rest. A very small part of you believed that the peanut might be magic and might allow me to speak with you. I squeezed myself through that crack."

Her explanation makes so much sense to me that it scares me. I want to wake up.

"I'm afraid I can't let you do that," she says. "If you awoke, I'd be at your mercy, and we can't have that. I'm much too important."

"What do you want from me?"

She grins. "I'm sure Nabelung already told you. That was part of the deal."

"You want me to be your servant."

"I want you to be and I need you to be. In the waking, I'm 93 years old. I don't remember who I am most of the time."

"You want me to take care of you?"

"Basically."

"I used to be a nutritionist, not a nurse. I wouldn't know how to—"

"No, here. I want you to take care of me here."

"Oh."

"You're a very unique man, Tomas. Most people hide from their pain.

But you. You bathe in it like it's a hot spring. Not that you enjoy it like you would a hot spring. Sorry, I'm not very good at metaphors."

"It's okay."

"What I'm trying to say is that your nightmares are beautiful, and I need your suffering much more than you do."

"No," I say. I'm still scared of her alright, but I'm more frightened of the prospect of giving away my pain.

It's who I am.

"The problem for you, Tomas, is that while I'm here I can control... well, next to everything. And, I know what you're afraid of."

I laugh so hard the room shakes. "I'm living my fears every day of my life. You couldn't make it any worse."

She shakes her head, and light dances on her gliding hair. "I can see how you'd think that. I used to be a lot like you before my brain gave out and I lost the connection with my past. But you're wrong."

"I find that very hard to believe."

"You're not the first." She disappears.

It was, of course, all just a dream. Now I'm back home in the wild where I belong.

That's right. I live in the jungle and forage for berries and nuts and hunt wild boar with my trusty spear named Sir Stabs-a-lot. The smells and the waterfalls of these parts are to die for. The caves are just deadly.

If you saw me praying over this bloody bunny rabbit I just bludgeoned to death with a river stone, you might assume I was an eccentric before abandoning my old life. You might guess it was my life-long dream to live this kind of life.

You'd be wrong.

Some desires are beyond simple dreaming. Sometimes you don't know what you really want until you have it.

Sometimes you survive a plane crash and before the rescuers show up, you realize the thunderbird that flew into the engine was actually a blessing in a feathery disguise.

So you stay.

I'm chomping on raw bunny organs when a photograph falls from the sky and hits the ground in front of me with a bellowing thud. I see them there, in that frozen smidgen of time. She's wearing a t-shirt that says "I LOVE MY BABY" and his says "I LOVE MY MOMMY." I made those shirts on some strange whim the night before Mother's Day. I burned my thumb on the iron and sucked it like a baby. This made me laugh amidst the pain.

The memory flashes in my mind for an instant, like I flipped on a light bulb that reveals so much and then burns out.

A horrible feeling attacks me. It's a feeling with claws and teeth and a sharp tail and breath of fire. I imagine the beast in the cave that I know is there but've never seen.

Here I am, living this life, and they're not. BABY and MOMMY.

If I sucked my thumb now, I wouldn't laugh or smile. I'd curl up in a fetal position on the jungle floor and cry myself to sleep.

The photograph catches fire.

And me with it.

It was, of course, all just a dream. Now I'm back home in the wild where I belong.

I may be wrong about this, but I think I dreamt of the cave. I think I wandered too close to the darkness and the beast dragged me inside by my right foot. He towed me through tunnels. He showed me glowing petroglyphs on the walls created a long time ago.

Created by me.

I look down at my feet, and a green stem snakes up from the forest floor. A red flower explodes into bloom. I feel like shielding my eyes, but I can't move.

Shapes begin to form in the petals. A woman and a boy.

The trick isn't to stop seeing them. It's to ignore them without looking away.

But I can't.

I remember.

It was, of course, all just a dream. Now I'm back home in the wild where I belong.

An almost orgasmic sense of relief gushes inside me. I release the horrible feeling that ravaged me, because whatever I was dreaming about, whatever happened inside the cave, it wasn't real.

Then I remember.

I remember everything.

"Jade," I say.

She steps out from behind a tree.

"I'll be your slave," I say.

"Servant," she says.

Sure I'm saddling her chest, holding down her arms as she writhes and kicks, but don't get the wrong idea. She's the one in control.

Green goop spurts from my eyes, nose, mouth in a constant stream onto Jade's agonizing face. The liquid burrows into her orifices. It dives into her mouth with every sputtering scream.

I think the word toxin. Then I don't.

After a while, she stops struggling. She trembles.

When I can't excrete anymore, I release her, lie on the floor, and attempt to cry. I'm too empty though. I'm numb.

A moment later, I'm standing in a hallway with Jade at my side. As far as I can tell, the corridor stretches on forever in both directions. Suddenly I feel very small.

"This is much better," Jade says. "Thank you." Her eyes shower me with a gentle radiance.

"You're welcome," I say, almost meaning it.

She takes my hand and we walk. Candles interspersed evenly on the walls light our way. The flames lean toward us as we pass.

"Her name is Aalia," Jade says.

"I don't want to do this," I say, and mean it.

"This isn't about you, Tomas. She needs us."

The door beside me swings open and Jade shoves me inside. I go for the door, but they're curtains now.

"Stay away from me," someone says, behind me. Aalia, I'm guessing.

I turn around and find her sitting on a bed, hugging her legs.

The old me wouldn't have crept toward her with a dark energy buzzing on his skin. The old me believed that the human body was a sanctuary, and a mystical one at that. He hugged his wife and son even when they weren't around.

This was me.

Now he's gone.

Aalia screams and runs out the bedroom window into the night.

I chase after her.

I chase her through a field of corn, which always points me in the right direction. I chase her through ancient ruins, and the symbols on the stones transform into arrows. She's betrayed at every turn.

There is no escape.

I corner her in a room without any windows or doors.

"Please don't hurt me," she says, crying.

"I won't," I want to say, but I don't believe that. I've done much worse.

The cloud of dark power around me seizes her as I approach. It grips and strangles and squeezes her mind.

I tower over her, not myself, but her husband. Her father. Whoever I am, I'm going to destroy her.

I touch her.

She screams and punches me in the gut. Hard.

I fly backwards, crashing and tumbling through wall after wall. Artifacts and corn whirl around me. They nip at my skin. When this world stops spinning, I'm back in the hallway and I have one hell of a stomachache.

I think of probiotics and chamomile tea. Then I don't.

"Sorry," Jade says. "I didn't know Aalia had that in her. No, that's not true. I knew it was there, I just didn't know she'd let it out yet. Anyway. Good job. She may leave him now in the waking."

I lift my shirt. My stomach expands and contorts into the shape of a hairbrush.

"What is this?" I say.

Jade kneels and pats my stomach. I yelp with pain. "It's sort of a difficult thing to put into words," she says. "At least for me. But what I can tell you is that the gap between you and Aalia, between your feelings and hers, is just an illusion. I create these illusions, so I know what I'm talking about."

I try vomiting, but I can't. "Are you going to take it out?"

"What's inside you is real, Tomas. It's yours to deal with. But I can help you."

A door opens.

I glance at my son through the rearview mirror. He chomps the head off a marshmallow chicken.

"Marshmallows used to be a medicine, you know," I say. "This was back when they added an extraction of the marsh mallow plant to the ingredients. Marsh mallow juice is great at healing wounds, boosting the immune system, and suppressing coughs."

"It tastes good," my son says.

I smile and look at my wife, like I often do when I smile. But she's asleep. Her hands rest on her lap, gripping a hairbrush. I smile again and turn my attention to the road.

A lost kitten poster flutters on a streetlight up ahead. I stare.

Suddenly, a chthonic force seizes me and squeezes my chest.

The voice says, "You are doomed."

I am doomed.

Fear closes in on me from all angles.

The light is red, but I can't move. My right foot remains pressed against the pedal.

It may look like I'm in control, but I'm not. I'm helpless.

"Stop doing this to me, Jade," I say.

"Don't blame me," Jade says, sitting in the back seat with my son.

This is how it happens. These are the moments before the truck hits. These are the moments that last an eternity.

"Why did I go through the light?" I say, crying, frozen. "Why didn't I stop?"

"Because you weren't paying attention," Jade says. "You were looking at that poster, thinking about your childhood cat, Snappy."

"Should they die for such a little mistake?"

"No. But they did. They will again if you keep this up."

"I don't know how to stop!"

"You can't stop."

There is no escape.

I see the presence in the approaching truck. He's the shadow of a man. A void that I created because I didn't know how to stop.

Now I do.

I slam on the brakes, and the truck comes to a screeching stop, just in time to avoid hitting my car, my family, and me.

I'm back in my car now, driving, safe.

"I'm sorry," I say. "I've been away for so long."

My wife laughs. "We've seen you every night, Tomas."

Jade touches the back of my head. I remember. My wife is right. I've dreamt of them hundreds of times since they left the world.

I want to say, "I love you," but for now I vomit out the window, and leave a trail of green behind us. A green that eats away at the asphalt and seeps deep into the ground.

That was me.

Now he's gone.

BABY EDWARD

THERE'S MORE THAN one way to kill a dream.

My dream is a baby boy named Edward and he's not allowed in the house. He lives in the VW Bus in my backyard. I keep the windows closed and the doors locked, which doesn't serve any real purpose, obviously. But I like to keep the key on a chain around my neck. I like to wear it under my dress shirt, coat, and tie. When I first put it on in the morning, the metal's cold against my chest. By the time I'm tapping at my keyboard, inventing new ways to politely coerce resources from suspecting citizens, I'm cold on the inside. Anytime I want, I can put the key in the lock, twist, and end this. But I don't. You might ask, where's the mother during all this? Well, I hate to burst your predictable bubble, but there is no mother.

I made Edward.

And he's mine.

Mine.

Harboring resentment is a great way to meet women. Try it. Sit down in your least favorite bar, let your eyes glaze over, frown, and put up your walls. The kind of walls you'd need to contain a plague, because most likely, that's what you are.

Now, see who comes knocking.

"Hi," Annabelle says.

I'm not psychic. She's wearing a nametag.

Well, maybe I am a little psychic.

"You're Ed," she says.

"How do you know that?" It's ridiculous, but I look down at my shirt to make sure I'm not wearing a nametag also.

"I remember you," she says. "About ten years ago I was visiting San Francisco and I heard you sing. We talked for about thirty seconds before I left. I wanted to talk with you more, but I was intimidated and shy. It's strange. I'm not usually good at remembering faces."

"Why did you want to talk to me?"

"Because your songs touched me, Ed. I told you that. Remember?" I don't.

Honestly, I don't even remember being in San Francisco.

"I remember," I say.

"You don't have to lie to me."

"Sorry."

She laughs. Maybe the way I used to laugh before my VW became a cage.

"Do you ever get the feeling that a storm is coming, a bad one, and you hope to God you're wrong, and then you are wrong and you're disappointed?" This is sort of what I want to say, except I want to scream it without any words. Gutturally. Instead, we talk about her job as a manicurist, or stuntwoman, or whatever it is she's saying.

If you heard the crying I'm listening to, you'd get a portable hacksaw from your basement too. You'd cut a hole in the side of the Bus so that you could insert a bottle.

An hour ago, I was in the bathroom, minding my own perverted business, and it started.

Actually, I'm guessing it began a while ago, before I heard any of the sobs. It's one of those cries that starts out silent and then bursts. The buildup has been going on for months. Maybe even years.

After my hard-on melted away, I tried burying my head in a pillow. I tried earplugs. I tried television, ice cream, a good book, a bad book. I tried cleaning and remembering my childhood and burning some old photographs. I tried driving around in my new BMW and keeping an eye out for the homeless.

I even tried not giving a shit.

Nothing works.

So I'm here, with this bottle and formula and cold sweat.

My head is killing me. I feel like fighting back.

"Just drink the damn milk," I say.

The crying stops.

I hear sucking.

The relief you expect me to feel is really nausea and a trick-fart that turns out to be quite a bit of diarrhea.

Good thing I'm not wearing my good pajamas.

The secret to a man's heart isn't food or sex. Annabelle and I have already shared those together, but they're not what keeps me from running away.

That's what I do, by the way. I run and I hide, the way I did when I was a kid, except it's not a game anymore. At least not a fun one.

I used to drive, searching for a place where I could be, for lack of a less cheesy sentiment, happy. A place where I could smell my lyrics in the air, and other such nonsense. I searched for a magical place. But I ended up here, of course, because real magic doesn't exist.

Enough of my bitching.

"How did you lose your leg?" I say.

"Trampoline accident." She pauses. "Sorry, that's a stupid joke."

"No it's not. I didn't know you were joking, so I didn't laugh."

"How could I lose my leg on a trampoline?"

"I don't know. It could get caught on the side."

"And then what? The force of the jump rips me in two?"

"I don't know."

She laughs. Maybe the way I used to before I started taking drugs. The legal kind, anyway.

"It was a car accident," she says.

"I'm sorry."

"You probably don't know this, but as soon as I said car accident, your face released a lot of tension."

"It did?"

"I used to be offended when I saw that in people. But instead of getting pissed off all the time, I decided to try to understand what was going on. I may be wrong, but my theory is that people don't like unexpected tragedy. Car accidents cause over a million deaths every year, and it doesn't matter, because it's normal. Like war is normal. Like malnutrition in Africa. Like... is that a dying animal outside?"

No. "I'll go check."

I present the food on my flattened palm, the way I did at the petting zoo when I was a kid. The first time I ever fed a goat, I was terrified that he'd chomp off my fingers, and I'd never be able to play piano again.

A similar terror molests my neck, my back, my stomach.

Ed won't drink milk anymore.

"Just eat the damn cereal," I say.

The difference between this feeding and the one at the petting zoo is that this time my fears are justified. Tiny sharp teeth rip open my flesh and clamp down on my bone. I scream and yank as hard as I can, but only manage to further mangle my index finger.

Ed yanks back, and pulls my arm deeper into the hole I cut in the side of the Bus. We play tug-of-war for a while.

"Let me go!" I say.

He doesn't.

I kick the Bus as hard as I can, and it must startle him, because he lets go.

I kick the Bus again before walking away.

Minutes later, I'm in bed all patched up.

"What happened to you?" Annabelle says.

"I accidentally smashed my finger with the car door."

"I'm sorry," she says. Relieved.

Annabelle whistles while putting on her leg. She's tone-deaf.

"Do you ever feel it?" I say.

"What?" she says.

"Your leg. The missing one. What's that called when you can feel it?"

"Phantom limb. Yeah. My phantom used to be really painful. It felt like my leg was on fire almost all the time."

"I'm sorry." There's no relief in my face.

"Nothing really helped until I started using the mirror box. It's exactly what it sounds like. A box and mirrors. I put my good leg in one hole and my phantom in the other. With the mirror, it looked like I had two good legs. So I moved the phantom in sync with the reflection of my good leg and tricked part of my brain into believing I was controlling the phantom. The reason why my phantom hurt in the first place was because my mind considered it stuck. I had to set it free."

By now we're in the kitchen. The key against my chest feels colder than usual. Or maybe I'm running a fever.

"What happened to all the food in the fridge?" Annabelle says.

"I accidentally left the door open and a lot of it went bad." I pause. "No, that's a lie. I can't keep lying to you. I'll show you what's going on."

"Good," she says, as if she's been waiting for these words. Maybe she has.

I take her hand, and lead her out of my present, into my past. We walk over the neatly-trimmed lawn, past the pawn-shaped fountain and the gnome-infested garden, to the corner of the yard exploding with weeds and wildflowers. It may only take a few moments to get here, but it's not an easy path to travel with someone else. I squeeze Annabelle's hand to keep myself from running away. She doesn't complain.

"In there," I say. I point. "He's in there."

The windows of the Bus are tinted, so she leans in close, and cups her hands around her eyes.

She's looking in more than a car, you know. I lived in this car. And even died a little.

When she returns to face me, she says, "It's just a guitar."

"You're a guitar," I say.

"What?"

"Sorry. I was being defensive."

"It's OK."

There's nothing wrong with her eyes, you know. She's just not looking the right way.

I want to tell her about Edward. I want to take off my bandages and show her my wounds. I want to let her hold my key. I would do these things, but there's a big problem.

I'm not on stage. A hundred thousand fans aren't singing the words with me. I'm only Ed.

So we go back inside.

Through the tinted glass, I see a dark form scampering about the seats. He's growling.

"No," I say. "No more food, Edward."

But he's not a good boy, like I used to be. He doesn't know when to stand down. So he slams his head against the wall, over and over.

"Stop that, Edward," I say.

He yelps with every blow.

Blood thrashes my innards.

"I'm not going to help you anymore, Edward," I say. "You're nothing but a nuisance."

He won't stop. I hear cracking.

I punch the window with my bad hand and scream.

At this point I realize that he's not trying to get my attention. He's after Annabelle.

When she peeked in before, he must have seen the kindness in her eyes. He knows she would feed him.

"It's no use, Edward," I say. "Annabelle slept through the last earthquake, and she'll sleep through you."

I smile, because I think I have him. I think, for a few fleeting moments, that he's going to lie on the seat, close his eyes, and suck his thumb.

Instead, he begins devouring the seats. His sharp little teeth tear at the upholstery, lacerate the metal, mutilate the seatbelts. He chews and swallows. Inhales.

"You're not getting any nutrients from that, Edward," I say.

He doesn't care.

If your girlfriend surprises you with a romantic candle-lit picnic, you can't tell her it's a horrible idea. You can't tell her that the blanket is too close to the weeds and the Bus and you-know-who. I guess you could tell her all this, but she's gazing at you, tickling inside you with her phantom toes.

So you say, "Thank you, Annabelle."

I see him staring through the window, drooling. He smiles, and I attempt to hide my fear with a smile of my own.

"I wish I could see the world through your eyes, Ed," Annabelle says.

"Why would you say that?" I say.

"Because you see such beauty around you."

"What I see is grotesque. I don't mean you."

"Your songs aren't grotesque."

"My songs aren't about the world. They're about the world in my head."

"What's the difference?"

An enormous hand crashes through the side of the Bus and wraps around Annabelle's torso.

She looks at me with relief on her face, as if she's always known it would come to this. Maybe she has.

As Edward pulls her into the darkness, I dive forward and try to grab her foot, but of course it's only a phantom, and my hand passes right through.

"Let her go, Edward!" I say.

I try to climb in through the hole, but a blubbery leg pushes me backwards. I punch, kick, and bite, the way I never did when I was a kid. I was a good boy.

It doesn't help.

I try to yank the chain off my neck, but it doesn't break, so I lift it off instead. I put the key in the lock, twist. It's time to end this.

Immediately a pudgy arm thrusts out of the driver's door and causes me to tumble onto the picnic candles. I go for the passenger door. This time I dodge the arm that darts at me. I open the door to the backseat and get kicked in the shoulder.

All of Edward's arms and legs hang outside of the Bus now, like he's some headless turtle.

I lift the hood.

There he is. He's eaten the engine. I know that's not all he's eaten.

"Open your mouth, Edward," I say. "Spit her out."

He doesn't respond.

"Spit her out!"

I reach down and try to open his mouth with my fingers, wounds and all. He won't even budge.

When I try to use my key, he bites it in half.

I slam the hood shut and return to the picnic blanket to think. Part of it's on fire, but I let it burn.

My head is killing me. I feel like surrendering.

I feel like lying on the grass, closing my eyes, and sucking my thumb.

Instead, I walk behind the Bus. Edward's penis dangles out of the exhaust pipe, and I open the back door. I know what I have to do.

If Edward won't let me in, then I'll force myself inside.

I do.

My journey gets a lot easier when I realize I don't have to fight anymore. It's time to let go. My body surges forward, twisting and turning through the intestines, but it doesn't matter which way I go, because I'm going to end up with Annabelle.

No matter what.

She may be shredded to pieces, of course, depending on whether or not Edward swallowed her whole. I may only have a few moments to grieve over her remains before the stomach acid melts my flesh.

And that's OK.

Finally, I reach the stomach. I reach Annabelle. She's alive.

We embrace, and stay that way.

Edward starts crawling, the Bus like armor around him.

The movement gently rocks me and Annabelle from side to side.

It's warm in here. Comfortable. Intimate.

I feel closer to Annabelle than I've ever felt to anyone, including myself. But we don't speak, me and her.

We don't need to.

I'm excited, because I know where we're going. We're going to a place where we can be happy. Where I can smell my lyrics in the air, and other nonsense. Where magic is real.

Edward vomits us up, and we sit amidst the chunky bowls of my old home-sweet-home.

This is just an ordinary park, but my girlfriend is alive. Edward seems happy, lying on the grass with his eyes closed, gnawing on a squirrel. I pick up my upchucked guitar. Annabelle may not be a hundred thousand adoring fans, but I'm coated with puke, and she still kisses me. French.

So I play.

THOSE BELOW

SAY YOU'RE LOST in the hustle-bustle of the local farmer's market in search of some shiny bibelot for your girlfriend, and you find your mother mouth-to-mouth with a man who isn't your father. In fact, he's nothing like your father. He's skinny and shaggy and short. You tell yourself that if he at least looked like your father, you could stomach the scene. Deep down you know that's not true.

And maybe that's not how it happens. Maybe you track her down. Maybe you climb the fruitless mulberry in front of their house and that's how you cut your leg. Maybe you bought yourself some night-vision goggles off of eBay. Maybe you're watching and waiting, and when you finally do see them together, in their bedroom, naked, you drop a bomb of vomit onto an unsuspecting yard gnome below.

You think, "Get your fucking hands off my mother."

But she's not your mother, is she? She used to be. Before she moved in here. Before she changed her name. Before the funeral.

Say this was your mother, and this is your life. You'd be here too, like me. You'd hear about Porter from a friend of a friend, and you'd show up at his doorstep with a hundred bucks and a wrenching knot in your gut.

Porter opens the door. "Yeah?"

I open my mouth, but nothing comes out.

"You're Hadley?" he says.

"Yeah."

"Alright. Come in."

I follow him inside. My mind spins, but I still notice that his home is a shitty place. Every step and my feet crunch down on trash and squish on soggy carpet. Lines of duct tape patch a few holes in the wall, but most are left gaping. I stop breathing through my nose before I have time to identity the sour stench assaulting the air.

He takes me to an empty room. At this point, the walls are more hole than wall. Under more relaxed circumstances I would crack up over such irony as the tarp on the floor, but I'm more in the mood for weeping.

"You brought the money?" he says.

I nod and hand him the bill.

He gives it back. "Not until after."

"Oh."

He takes another look at the money. "That's a hundred dollar bill, huh?"

"Yeah."

"I don't think I've seen one before. In person, I mean."

"Oh." I stuff the thing in my pocket, almost violently.

"Should I get undressed?" he says, and starts for his belt.

"I'm not here for...that."

"I know, man." He grins. "Just some people like me naked when they're doing it. I don't mind either way."

I consider this. "Keep your clothes." Part of me, though, wants to give the other answer. The thought makes me shudder.

"Whatever floats your boat." He kneels. "Whenever you're ready."

I take a step forward, and then pause. "Is this going to hurt you?"

"Fuck, man, what do you care?"

"I care."

"You say that now. Let's see if you ask me again in five minutes."

"Maybe I'm not your normal clientele."

He sighs. "No, we don't feel much pain, so clear your fucking conscience."

"Are you just telling me that or do you mean it?"

He runs his hand down his face. "Look, man. You can either do this or go home. But no one ever goes home, so just face the fucking music and get on with it."

So I do.

I start off by slapping him hard across the face, and go from there. Five minutes later, I'm not asking, "Is this hurting you?"

Five minutes later, I'm straddling his chest, smashing his mangled face in with my bloody fists, over and over and over. He's shouting, "Stop it!" and I'm loving every second of it.

Hafwen's nickname is Zippy. She likes to skip and sing about the dishes as she's washing them and write poetry with waterproof paper in the rain. She'll call me up just to tell me that she's discovered the name for those imprints left in the skin when you press it against a textured surface too long. A frittle.

So when I see her sitting cross-legged on my bed, motionless, not frowning, but not smiling, I know something's wrong.

I sit beside her and kiss her. "What's up, Haf?"

She doesn't look at me. "I have to tell you something."

My insides erupt. I'm afraid.

I'm afraid her feelings for me were just a frittle in her heart and now she wants to end what we have before I even have the chance to tell her I love her.

"Tell me," I say. I try to sound brave, but I fail.

"My mom," she says. "She's a Remade-American."

"Oh," I say. "I didn't know Cambree wasn't your real mom."

"No, Hadley. Cambree is my real mom. She's a Remade-American."

"Oh god...I'm so sorry. When did this happen? I saw her last week."

"No, Hadley. She was a Remade since before she married my dad."

"Oh."

"I'm a Remade, Hadley."

"But..." I can't think of anything else to say except, "You don't look like one of them."

"One of them?"

"I'm sorry. I..."

She looks at me now. "I should've told you before we started going out, but...I liked you so much. I wanted you to get to know me first before you...you know...decided."

"Oh."

"I told myself that I wasn't lying to you, because I never said that I was alive, but keeping this from you was deceitful and I'm sorry. I understand if you're angry at me. I'm angry at me too."

"I'm not angry," I say, and that's true. I'd have to be feeling anything to feel angry.

"I don't know if that's a good sign or a bad one," she says.

"Me neither."

She puts her face in the bowl of her hands and makes crying sounds. No tears come out, obviously.

I almost put my arm around her, but I don't.

"I can't keep living this way, Hadley," she says. "I'm a Remade. I'm tired of hiding it."

I want to tell her, "Don't worry."

I want to tell her, "I'll love you no matter what."

But I fail.

I thought Hafwen was happy before. But she tells me she wasn't. She says she was smiling on the outside and crying on the inside.

Now, she cries a lot.

Now, she's pale, because she's stopped wearing makeup. She's cold, because she's stopped wearing heated clothing. Her hair is white, because she's stopped dyeing it. She looks dead, and says she's the happiest she's ever been.

I should be happy for her. Instead, I keep thinking about how someone else used to inhabit her body. I can't look at her the same way anymore.

She's used.

Second-hand.

Impure.

She says a lot of Remade girls try to pass for living, because they're ashamed of who they are. They buy into the whole natural is ugly paradigm. But natural isn't ugly, she says. Death isn't ugly.

Whether she's right or not, I don't know.

If there is a beauty in death, I don't want to see it.

I hate death. I hate that my mom died of thirst in a ditch on the side of the road. People drove by, but they didn't see her. They didn't hear her.

Now when Hafwen stands right in front of me, I try to look through her. When she talks to me, I try to tune out her voice. Deep down, I know she doesn't deserve this kind of treatment. I also know that Porter doesn't deserve the beatings I give him every Tuesday morning.

I just don't care.

"Animal brains have to be illegal," I say. I say it with conviction, but I don't really know what I'm talking about. I defend the living and the systems controlled by the living only because doing otherwise would feel like a betrayal. "They're a gateway to human brains."

Hafwen laughs. "You really think there are hordes of Remades out there feasting on the brains of the living?"

"I don't know," I say. "It could happen."

"Hadley, animal brains are illegal because Remades eat them. They make us feel good."

"Have you ever eaten any?"

"No, but that's not the point. The point is, prisons are filled with Remades, and most of them are there just because they've eaten animal brains. The government sells these prisoners to corporations to use for manual labor, and every living person involved makes a lot of money. Doesn't this seem wrong to you?"

"I guess," I say. "But you have to admit. Violent Remade crime is a big problem."

"If you read the statistics, you'd know that violent living crime is an even bigger problem. It only seems like a Remade problem because the media publicizes Remade crime a lot more often. A lot."

"I don't want to talk about this anymore."

"But we are talking about it, Hadley. It's important to me."

A few days ago, Hafwen told me the story of her parent's divorce. I expected her to say that her mother lied about being a Remade and that when her father found out the truth, he left her.

But that's not how it happened.

Her father, Barry, knew that her mother was a Remade from the very beginning. He was an activist for Remade rights and that's how they met in the first place. He loved Cambree and he wanted to start a family with her. So they had a baby. Her name was Bronwyn. Since she was born from a Remade mother, Barry and Cambree knew that at any time she could pass away and be Remade with a new personality. This happened when Bronwyn was 19 years old. Barry loved Bronwyn, and refused to connect with Hafwen in any meaningful way, and all the while he blamed Cambree for his daughter's death. One day he left for work and never came home again.

Now, this story buzzes in my head. I know that Hafwen's just looking for some living person to listen to her. To understand her. To say, "You're right. These things are very unfair."

But instead I say, "I'm going to bed."

This is our coffee-shop, Hafwen's and mine. Neither of us drink coffee but we enjoy the comity and the photographs of dancing mannequins on the walls.

Today, I don't invite her. I've never seen a Remade in here before, though I tell myself the reason I don't call her is because I need some alone time.

A man and a woman at the next table converse in loud whispers.

I stare at my book like I'm reading.

"I'm no racist," the woman says. "But they have no legal right to be here."

"I say send them back to where they came from," the man says. "Start paving all the cemeteries and let that be the end of it."

At least I'm not them. I don't want to get rid of the Remades. I'm all for equal rights. Hell, I'm even dating one of them.

I'm not a terrible person. So why do I feel like such a monster?

Minutes later I'm in my car making a call.

"Porter?" I say.

"Yeah," he says. "Hey, man."

"Do you want to hang out?"

"Hang out?"

"Yeah. We could go bowling or something."

"I hate bowling."

"Whatever you want."

"I don't know, man. I don't usually hang out with clients."

"Come on."

"Alright."

Fifteen minutes later, and I'm in a Remade bar. My mind spins, but I still notice that this is a shitty place. Like it hasn't been cleaned since it opened. Maybe that's true.

The waitress, who's either a living person or one of those Remades who buy into the natural is ugly paradigm, hands me my chai, and gives Porter a wad of tin foil.

"Thanks, man," he says to the girl.

She smiles and walks away.

Porter unwraps the foil.

"What is that?" I say.

"Brains," he says.

"I know that. I mean, what kind?"

"Human."

"Oh." I swallow.

"I'm just fucking with you, man. They're pig. Want to try some?"

"No!" I'm louder than I expect.

"Calm down, man."

I try.

Porter nibbles at the brains. He trembles.

After a few sips of my tea, I say, "Is it really so bad being dead?"

"What do you mean?" he says, gazing at his hands.

"I mean, why do so many Remades eat brains? Is it such a horrible existence?"

"No, man. Being dead is cool."

"Then why do you eat brains?"

His expression changes to one that I've never seen on him before. It's one of the looks my mother used to give me, when she was disappointed in me, but showed sympathy at the same time. "Figure it out yourself, man," he says, very quietly.

"Fuck you!" I say, standing.

"Let go of me."

I realize my hand is squeezing his arm. My other hand, it's in a fist.

"I think you should go, man," he says.

Part of me wants to stay and beat the non-living shit out of him. I want to blame him. Not just for how I'm feeling right now, but for everything. My mother's death. The state of the world.

Everything.

Instead, I release him and say, "Yeah."

Say you're lost in the orange groves behind your apartment complex because you're not ready to go home again, and you find three guys dragging a tied-up young woman toward a hole in the ground, with three shovels nearby. They're alive and she's not. You tell yourself that if they were dead and she wasn't, the scene wouldn't be so disturbing, because it's supposed to be the dead who do things like this. Deep down you know that's not true.

You think, "Get your fucking hands off her."

Say all of this happens. You'd be here too, like me. You'd crouch down behind the nearest trunk you can find, waiting and watching, with a wrenching knot in your gut.

For a moment I consider racing out into the clearing, bellowing and swinging my fists. But these guys, they're not like Porter. They'd fight back. They'd kill me.

So I watch them bury the poor girl. I listen to her muffled screams.

They dump her in the hole and start shoveling.

They say things like, "You like that dirt in your face, don't you, bitch?" and "Fucking zombie whore."

I try to study their faces, so that I can identify them later, but it's so dark. And I'm crying too much.

When they finish with the dirt, they pound the backs of their shovels against the grave, over and over and over. They laugh, and high-five.

Finally, they leave.

I dive onto the ground and start digging with my bare hands.

What I'm uncovering isn't just a young dead girl.

From deep within myself, I pull out a truth that I've always known but never wanted to admit. Remades don't eat brains because of the pain of being dead. The real pain comes from how the living treat them. How I treat them.

I pull her out of the hole. I remove the gag.

She looks at me with fear in her eyes.

I'm afraid she's going to scream.

I'm afraid she thinks I'm one of them.

But her face changes. It's one of the looks my mother used to give me, after I did something bad and then made things right. "Thank you," she says, very quietly.

I put my arm around her, and in my heart I'm embracing Hafwen at the same time.

I see her when I close my eyes.

She's beautiful.

I'm ready to go home.

DEVOURED

I JAB THE carving fork into my thigh, and start cutting off another slice.

"Thicker than that," you say.

So I move the knife over another inch, and saw through the flesh and bone.

It's painful, of course. But the worst part is that you don't hold my hand or touch my eyes with your gaze. You only stare at the piece of me that's slowly becoming yours.

"Is this good?" I say, and hold out the circle of meat.

"We'll see," you say. "Feed me."

"What shape would you like?"

"A car."

"I'm not sure if I know how to make it like that."

You point your finger at my face. "Just do it, Jessica! Or I'll find someone else who can."

And so I attempt to mold the meat into a car. It takes me a good two hours, but I finally get the job done.

"Do you know what time it is?" you say, tapping your watch.

"7 o'clock," I say.

"That's right. And I'm fucking starving."

I uncover the platter with the flesh car on top.

You study it for a while, frowning. "The tires don't look very realistic, but I guess it's alright."

"Thanks," I say.

You eat the car. You like me to watch, so that's what I do.

"How does it taste?" I say.

"You're not as fresh as you used to be."

"I'm sorry."

"Well, nevermind. I'm finished. Let's go to bed."

"Would you carry me?"

"Fine." You grab me, and toss me on the bed upstairs. "You know, you look like a fucking idiot without any legs."

"I know."

"Stay over there. I don't want you to bleed on me."

I'd like to move closer to you, of course, but I stay where I am.

And my leg continues bleeding, even in my dreams.

In the morning, you say, "I'd like some head meat for breakfast."

"OK," I say, the way I always say, "OK."

Because without you, I'm nothing.

SCRATCH

MARGARET, ONE OF my least favorite wives, blocks the television as if anything she says is as interesting or witty as scripted dialogue crafted by professional writers; as if her smile with the chipped tooth is as enchanting as a celebrity's; as if I haven't seen this one a thousand times already."I have something special planned for you later," Margaret says. "It involves strawberries, handcuffs and a very lucky umbrella."

I laugh, because she expects me to.

"Be honest," she says. "Is that too kinky? Not kinky enough?"

"You know what, honey?" I say. "I'm not really feeling it tonight. I'm sorry."

"Not feeling it?"

"I don't think I can do this so...often anymore."

"Oh."

"I'd like to. It's just that my body isn't responding the way that it used to."

"I see."

She should walk away. Run, really.

But instead, she steps closer. She can't help herself. Not because of gravity or magnetism or even attraction. It's because every night after she falls asleep, I sit beside her, and read to her from my notebook with the kitten on the cover. You probably don't know this, but that kitten was run over and killed and run over a few more times three days after that photograph was taken. And if you look close enough, with a magnifying glass would be best, you can see fear in the kitten's eyes. Part of him knows what's coming. Part of him isn't so innocent.

"Don't look so sad," I say. "Our relationship has evolved beyond the physical. I get so much more pleasure from talking to you now than touching you."

"You don't like touching me?" she says, closer.

"I do. Of course I do. But our bodies aren't what they used to be. We're not built for sex at this age. You can't have children anymore, so we've lost our physical appeal."

"I can get surgery," she says, on my lap now. "I can change."

"Yes, but you can't change into a younger woman. You can never get back what you lost."

She holds me tight. "I don't want to lose you."

"You won't," I say, and smile. "No matter what fades from our relationship, I'll always appreciate what we have. Always."

She squeezes me. She cries on me.

Then she folds into me like a hide-a-bed, and poof. She's gone.

"That's how you do it," I say.

Sonny pops his head out of the enormous vase where he was hiding and says, "I'm not sure exactly what you did, Mr. Grelding."

"Of course you're not sure," I say. "You're a student."

Look at him jumping out of that vase like some green-screened ninja. He thinks he's so great. Just because he's young and good looking and smarter than the average bear. I bet he's never traveled back and forth through time or fought in an intergalactic space war or saved the world from the apocalypse.

I bet he's even a virgin.

After setting down in the forest clearing, I unfasten my rocket pack and let it smash a couple of mushrooms or mice or whatever they were.

"Now I'm going to teach you how to have a baby," I say.

Sonny doesn't unfasten his rocket pack. It's heavy, and he's trying to prove his manliness to me because when he sees me, he sees his father, which is always a nice money maker.

"I didn't think you could have a child without a woman," he says.

"Without a woman?" I say. "Let me ask you something, Sonny. Are you retarded?"

"I take offense to that, Mr. Grelding. My cousin has autism."

"Autism is the same as retarded?"

"I wouldn't call anyone retarded. It's insensitive."

"I am insensitive, retard. The point is, of course you need a woman to have a baby. I have twelve inside me right now."

"Babies?"

"Women. Now pay attention."

I gather the best bits and pieces from each woman inside. Linda's math skills. Margaret's libido. Cindy's looks. Fran's obsessive perfectionism. On and on. I gather them and sculpt them into a little boy. As for the leftovers. Linda's ugliness. Margaret's weak stomach. Cindy's stupidity. Fran's compassion. On and on. I dump the scraps into a little girl.

Soon I'm bent over, heaving, vomiting hard on a wounded mouse that managed to drag itself from under my rocket pack.

I upchuck the boy first. The girl comes second. They're dripping with bile and I pull out my permanent marker and draw an X on the girl's forehead. I carry them both to the cage and lower them inside. I'm careful.

"With everything I put inside him, he'll be the next Einstein," I say. "Or at least the next Bill Gates."

"What will she be?" Sonny says.

"She'll be a meal for the beasts. You might not know this, but in beast society, human children, especially babies, are considered quite the delicacy. I give them a few surplus children and they raise my real children in exchange."

"But what's the point of having children if you're not going to raise them?"

"I take them back after they're older and less annoying. It's easier to assimilate them into human society than you might think. It just takes some tough love, and that's something I have a lot of."

His eyes twinkle, because he's hoping that part of me loves him.

And I keep his hope alive by smiling at him. He's pathetic.

I close the cage.

The troublesome part of having a wind up house is that you need to employ a fulltime winder and the turnover rate is 100%, what with the severe hand crippling. Other than the pesky paperwork and interviews, however, it's a blast.

Most people, I suppose, like to detach themselves from the suffering required to keep their opulent lifestyles up and running. Me, I like to watch, sitting in my comfiest chair, gobbling down popcorn.

"Nice work, Hans," I say, between chomps.

"Thank you, Mr. Grelding," Hans says. He's winding up the fireplace, which of course doesn't require any winding. Hans is probably smart enough to know this, but he turns the fake winding key anyway.

Sonny comes in and pulls a Rubic's cube out of a shopping bag. He holds it out to me.

"What?" I say. "I don't want it."

"You asked me to buy it for you," Sonny says. "You said you'd pay me back."

"I wouldn't ask for this. I hate games."

"I must have misheard you." Sonny puts the cube back in the bag.

Hans continues to the turn the key. His hands continue to wither and die.

"Sonny," I say. "We need to have a little talk. Sit down."

He does.

"First of all," I say. "I want you to know that I believe in you. Really, I do."

"Thank you, Mr. Grelding."

"You have the will to succeed in my program, but your body and mind are going to need a little extra help. I'm afraid I have to increase the cost of your tuition to cover the additional training time."

Sonny scoots closer to me. "I'm already too financially strained as it is,

Mr. Grelding. I'll work harder, I promise."

"It's not as simple as that, Sonny."

He moves closer.

"You can't make your flaws disappear by working hard," I say. "They're a deep-seated part of you, and these limitations don't make you a bad person. They make you special. I'm prepared to give you more of my time and energy to compensate for your special needs, but I need to be compensated in return. I don't think that's too much to ask."

Sonny should laugh in my face.

But instead, he sits closer. He can't help himself. Not because of respect or admiration or even fear. It's because every night after he falls asleep, I sneak into the guest room, and read to him from my notebook with the kitten on the cover. You might not know this, but I own a cat. He's small and stupid. Without me, he'd die for sure.

"I'll pay," Sonny says. He starts to hug me, but I stand and head for the kitchen.

"The microwave, Hans," I say.

"Right away, Mr. Grelding," Hans says.

I can tell he's in pain, and that's my pain in his hands. It's my childhood, my traumas. My house runs on suffering, and the whole situation makes me burst with laughter sometimes while I'm in the shower or stuck in traffic. Anywhere, really.

"Damn, I burned it," I say. "The microwave again please, Hans."

"Right away, Mr. Grelding."

The scratch is worse today. I can't say I'm surprised.

It all started a few days or weeks or was it months ago when my small and stupid cat approached me in my living room and clawed my leg for no apparent reason. When he headed for the door, I didn't chase him. I didn't kick him. In fact, I didn't dignify this trivial scraping with any response whatsoever.

I forgot the incident ever happened, and any time I remembered, I forced myself to forget again.

When I first noticed the thick yellow pus on the cut, I laughed.

Days or weeks or was it months passed, and the wound spread, snaking up my leg, around my genitals thank god, and up my stomach. The swollen stretch of skin burns and itches. It's infested with rancid boils spewing green ooze.

Obviously on some level, I should go to a doctor. But I can't. I can't let the cat win.

So I'm trying out another home remedy. Sooner or later I'll invent something that works. Today I drench the injured tissue with gasoline and industrial strength wasp spray. I scream for a while, which probably means it's working.

Before I'm done reapplying the bandages, a young woman enters my room. She points a spear at me and says, "You." She says this as if she's somebody, but she's not glamorous or delicate or skinny or passive in the least. She's nothing.

She slashes the blade across my chest, and I'm not very invulnerable when I'm not wearing my bionic exoskeleton.

I dip my finger in my blood. "Who are you?" I say.

"I'm your daughter," she says.

"I don't have any daughters."

"You left me to die, but a beast named Elina saved me from the others and raised me as her own. She told me who you were. I finally found you." She smiles.

I pick up the phone and try to call the police, but the phone isn't wound up.

"Hans!" I say. "Phone!"

Then I remember he quit earlier today. He even managed to give me the finger, despite his handicap. That was before he stole all the keys.

"Sonny!" I say. Then I remember he left to buy me a new chess set.

The girl swings and slices my arm.

And I do the only thing I can think of doing. I scramble over to my nightstand and read to her from my notebook with the kitten on the cover.

"You're unworthy," I say. "You're ugly. You're stupid. You're a failure. You're unlovable."

She growls at me, from the depth of what must be her soul or something just as frightening, and knocks the notebook from my hands. I know I shouldn't be scared of this nothing of a woman. I know she's small and stupid like my cat.

But I can't stop shaking.

"What do you want?" I say.

"I don't know yet," she says, and cuts my other arm.

"I can give you money."

"We don't use currency in beast society."

"I can try to be a real father to you."

"It's a little too late for that."

She moves fast and carves up my forehead. She draws an X.

I should walk away. Run, really.

But instead, I step closer. I can't help myself. Not because of duty or empathy or even love. It's because every night before I fall asleep, I think the things from my notebook with the kitten on the cover. You might not know this, but I'm not very happy.

I hold my daughter and say, "I can change."

She pushes me away. She lifts her spear and brings it down on me. She cuts off my bandages.

I look down at my body, and in my mangled rotting flesh, I see faces. Linda. Margaret. Cindy. Fran. On and on. They're squirming up my stomach, up my chest. They're smiling. They're chewing. I'm itching and scratching, and they're gnawing my finger with sharp chipped teeth.

Finally, the faces reach my head, my childhood, my traumas, and poof. I'm gone.

DOG

You SHOULD SEE this guy, with his black cape and his gargoyle face. He walks toward me like he's never tripped a day in his life. He's the sort of guy you would kill before disappointing.

You know the type.

He's your father, your teacher, your God.

And he would pass right by me if I didn't say, "Fuck you."

So I do.

He stops and I smile. "What did you say to me?" he says.

"I didn't say anything."

"I'm sure you did."

Of course he's sure. He's sure about everything, with shoes like that. He could stomp a horse to death with those horrors.

"Look at me when I'm talking to you," he says.

"I am," I say. "I'm looking at your feet."

He draws his sword. Of course he draws his sword.

"Do you know who I am?" he says.

"Someone who hears things on bridges," I say. Or maybe I just think it. It doesn't really matter.

He demands an apology, which is a courtesy not granted to me very often, and I'm guessing he's even more famous than I thought. With manners like that.

"Well, are you going to apologize or not?" he says.

"I'll apologize to your mother," I say.

I'm not really sure what that means, but like I said, it doesn't really matter at this point.

Our swords meet, fall in love, divorce and hate each other's guts.

I'm driving him back across the bridge, back toward the village or small town he came from. Back to the celebration in his honor, where everyone's drunk with delusion and feeling saved.

My arm doesn't know the first thing about sword-fighting, but I'm winning.

This is government-funded power versus year after year of arduous training.

The power always wins.

And it does, again.

The caped man doesn't say anything before he dies, though I imagine him saying, "Who are you?" And I say, "Fuck you."

When I was a kid I was afraid of bees, so I caught them in glass cups and left them out in the sun to die. Sometimes I set them free before it was too late. Mostly, I didn't.

Now I'm dragging a dead dog by the tail. I'm dragging her toward an apple tree under the full moon, because these are the three ingredients.

Dog, apple, moon.

That's all it takes.

"Where are we going?" my companion says. I forgot her name already, but I think it's some sort of flower.

"I told you," I say. "It's a surprise."

Rose laughs while not removing her blindfold. Obviously she's the sort of woman who gives you more than you deserve.

You know the type.

She's your mother, your lover, your whore.

"Take off your blindfold," I say.

Lily obeys. She screams and I smile.

"I'm not going to hurt you unless you run away," I say. "I only want you to be here with me. That's all. You don't have to do anything but be here."

"I want to go."

"I know you do." I point to a spot on the ground clear of rotten apples. "Sit there."

She doesn't.

"Sit there!"

She does.

I take out my knife, and Buttercup screams again. Then she tells me something about her sister and a birthday party and a hat she needs to buy.

Ivy won't last long in this world, with lies like that.

I get to work on the dog. Before I slice open her belly, I catch a glimpse of myself in the knife. Everything that was right about my old face is wrong about this one. My nose is too big. My lips are too small. And as for my skin, the mole below my eye looks like a hairy maggot trying to escape.

Daisy never would have come with me if I hadn't cursed her in her sleep. I remember wishing for the husband to wake up so that I could wave to him or wink at him before leaping out the window.

Now I'm yanking out organs with my gloves off. I toss them in a pile close enough to Marigold so that a bit of blood will splatter on her yellow dress. She's telling me something about a daughter I know she doesn't have. Something about pity.

"It's important that I use fresh apples," I say. "Rotten ones don't have the same effect."

I stuff the apples into the hollowed out dog. I fill her.

Sunflower heaves and vomits beside the mound of innards. I expected her to do this sooner, but life is full of surprises.

I sew the dog up. Almost immediately, she starts shaking. She whines. If you looked into her eyes, you could see her soul galloping back, but they never make it in time.

The dog foams at the mouth and the ass.

I approach Lilac. I hold out my hand. "Take it," I say.

She stares at my bloody palm. "Take what?"

"My hand."

She does.

I help her to her feet.

"Kiss me, then you can go," I say.

"What?" she says.

"Kiss me. Then you can go," I say again, or maybe I just grind my teeth.

She looks at me and the blood all over my arms. She glances at my face, because I have a habit of touching my head, and I'm sure there's blood there too. She watches the dog for a while as well, now a quaking mass of boiling flesh. The whining's only intensified with time. It's almost a howl.

The curse is enough to keep Hyacinth here, but not enough to make her kiss me. That, she has to do on her own.

She leans forward.

"No," I say. "I want you to hold me and kiss me. Properly. Then you can go."

She steps forward and wraps her arms around me, trembling like the dog.

Power always wins.

And my little Sweet Pea gives me my kiss.

Even after all their years of marriage, Smoke and Velvet still hold hands during dinner. I can't see evidence of this today, however, because I'm sitting at the table instead of below it. I'm a guest instead of a bored invisible enemy with itches he can't scratch because the movement might make too much noise.

"They act like they're causing us a minor inconvenience," Smoke says. "But people are starving."

"Not in front of Salmon," Velvet says.

Their little boy looks up from his plate. He's a lot younger than I was when I started out. Somehow, I don't care.

"We can't hide this from him," Smoke says. "Our village is better off than most, but it's only a matter of time. People are going to die."

"If only our people were smarter," I say. "Then we wouldn't suffer like this."

Smoke and Velvet stare at me.

"I'm kidding," I say. I laugh.

Velvet gives me a few weak chuckles, more than I deserve.

"We all know there's only one way to end the suffering," Smoke says. "We have to fight."

"We'd only suffer more," Velvet says. "You remember what happened the last time."

"We'll win if we're united."

"Rain, please talk some sense into my husband."

I shake my head. "I agree with him. We should kill them all."

"What happened to my pacifist brother?" Smoke says, and chortles.

"I murdered him and stole his face," I say.

After a few moments of silence, Velvet says, "Would anyone like dessert?"

"Me," Salmon says, and raises his hand.

"Do you have any apples?" I say.

A single word. That's all it takes.

And so a hairless dog bursts through the window and lunges at Velvet's neck. She falls onto her back. She claws at the beast as it ravages her, but she only manages to rupture a few boils.

The dog's already eating Velvet's face by the time Smoke reaches the other side of the table. He tackles the dog.

I take this time to reach under the table and retrieve my sword.

When I return to my spot, Smoke is without a nose and trying to say something to his son, who's curled up on the floor.

The dog finishes Smoke off with a few choice bites, then charges at the boy.

I lift my sword, wait, and slice the dog in half. The back half kicks itself across the floor into the unlit fireplace. The front half scurries toward Salmon, snapping and frothing, spilling rotten apple guts from its wound.

Sure I could use my sword to finish her off, but I decide to stomp her to death instead, with new shoes like these. They're horrors.

I approach Salmon, and the sound of the dog's back half scuttling around in the fireplace annoys me, though not enough for me to act.

I hold out my hand. "Take it," I say.

He does, crying like a baby.

"Everything's going to be alright," I say. "Uncle Rain will take care of you now."

My little Salmon hugs me and I smile.

Stump is one of them. He's also crusted over and as he twitches, bits and pieces of his outer layer tumble down his face. He smells like every liquid in his body has gone sour. Obviously, he's the sort of guy it's easy to keep alive, with flaws like that.

"Can I help you?" he says in the doorway, massaging a dull knife with his stained purple fingers.

"Asunder," I say.

A single word. That's all it takes, and he knows it's me.

He tosses the knife inside. "I'll get the case."

I wait outside, because I'm not going in there. I'd lose a piece of me that I could never get back.

Stump returns with the opened case. "What'll it be today?" He attempts a smile, and flakes from his face snow down on the glass bottles.

"You should consider bathing," I say. "You're going to scare away customers."

"Not you," he says.

I pick out three bottles. "I'll take these."

"That's too much," he says.

Of course it's too much.

"Two is too much," he says. "But I'll give you two. That's more than fair."

"Three."

"I can't."

I return the bottles. "I'll find someone else."

Stump's facial tremors die down. Then he bites a fingernail until he bleeds. "Take them," he says. "Let's just hurry this up. I'll meet you out back." He slams the door too close to my face, and I'll make him pay for that someday. Someday when he's old and I don't need him anymore.

I notice Salmon isn't in my shadow. "Come on."

"I want to go home," Salmon says.

I tell him not to worry. Or maybe I ignore him and walk around the house.

Stump is standing by the hole, naked and ready.

I cut my finger with a sharp memory. With the blood, I draw symbols on Stump's crispy chest. I write promises to spirits that I'll never keep, but I'll be fine. I'm not drunk with delusion when I say I'll always be fine.

"I have to pee," Salmon says.

I stab Stump through the heart and kick him into the hole. After I clean my sword, I get to work burying him.

Salmon cries. But soon enough, I'll get him to shut up for good.

"He'll come back," I say. "I promise."

For once, I'm not lying to the boy. Stump's life will come rushing back, and it's the rush that he's after. It's the rush that makes him a pathetic traitor to his own people.

"I have to pee," Salmon says, through his tears.

"Piss on his grave," I say, or maybe I only point.

Salmon pisses his pants instead.

"Come on," I say. "We're going."

But before that, I take out the bottle with the black liquid and dump it onto a potted plant. I only need the two.

Salmon doesn't squeak or squeal, even when the owl surges into flight beside us. I told him to stay quiet and he's quiet. Like a good boy.

Once we're through the window, I pour a bit of purple fluid onto every corner of this dusty attic. Salmon should be thankful that I brought him here instead of a cave, which is the traditional choice. I was tamed in a cave. I was carried inside in a burlap bag and lost more than a piece of me that I could never get back.

The purple fluid lights up in each corner. It smells like rotting fish, but it does the job.

"We can talk now," I say. I squat down so Salmon can drop off my back.

He doesn't.

"Get off," I say.

He does.

"I want to go home," he says.

"It's not safe there," I say. "There are dogs after you. You saw what the one did to your parents. And where there's one, there's a hundred. Or a thousand. It's hard to say exactly how many."

Salmon cries, hard.

"We've outrun them for now," I say. "But we can't keep running forever, can we? Real men stand and fight."

"I can't," he says, remembering the dog ripping off his father's nose, or something of the sort.

"You're right," I say. "Right now you don't stand a chance. We have to make you stronger."

So I hand him the bottle with the white pus inside. I tell him to drink it and he does. He doesn't even ask me what it is.

A blink later, his crying stops and I smile.

He touches his face. Even his tears have evaporated.

It's a start.

You should see the look on Salmon's face as I carry the dog closer.

He'd cry and scream and tremble if he could. He'd run away if he could take his eyes off her. His terror is silent and it's almost heartbreaking. Somehow, I don't care.

"Let me go," he says. Or maybe, "Let it go." It's hard to be sure, with a mind like this.

"Kill her," I say.

Salmon doesn't.

The little lost dog rests in my arms, cradled and calm. She trusts me more than I deserve.

"Kill her," I say.

Salmon doesn't, again.

I remember when I killed my dog. I remember the bones wriggling out of her mouth, and I remember the strange sounds she made. I remember the strange sounds I made.

My mentor, he looked at me with those terrible eyes, grinning, like he'd never lost a fight a day in his life.

Now I'm the one with horrors for eyes.

Now, finally, it's my turn.

"She wants to kill you," I say.

"She's not like that," Salmon says.

"They're all the same!" I say. "Kill her! Now!"

Salmon doesn't.

He's the sort of kid you want to beat into shape.

You know the type.

He's your son, your student, your slave.

I hold the dog close to Salmon's face, and he pushes her away. He also pushes out some of those precious feelings aching to come out.

The dog yelps, hard. Her flesh sizzles where Salmon touched her and only a hairless handprint of smoking tissue remains.

She doesn't trust me anymore.

I squeeze her tight.

"Let her go," Salmon says.

"Kill her," I say.

Once again, he doesn't. Instead, he does what I couldn't when I faced my dog in the cave. He holds back.

I take a step backward.

Part of me wants to lock him in a glass cage, and leave him out in the sun to die. The other part of me wants to win.

I throw the dog at him, and Salmon jumps out of the way. He doesn't chase after the dog. He doesn't rip her apart with the memory of his parents' death.

He picks up my sword.

He approaches me.

"The dog's that way," I say, and point.

But he doesn't turn around. Everything inside him should be screaming, "Dog!" but he's pointing the sword at me.

"Why was the sword under the table?" Salmon says.

I look around for a table, but don't see any.

Then I remember that Salmon's not really here. He's still in the dining room with his dying parents, and that's where he'll always be.

"You put the sword under the table," Salmon says.

"It's my sword," I say.

"You didn't have it when you came in," he says. "You put it there before. You knew what was going to happen."

"You're crazy."

"You killed them."

"Fuck you."

Salmon swings the sword at me and drives me back toward the wall. His arm doesn't know the first thing about sword-fighting, but it doesn't matter. He'll win.

Of course he'll win.

This is government-funded power in his little hands, and that's all it takes.

The power always wins.

I tell Salmon something about how he's like the son I never had. Something about pity.

Somehow, he doesn't care.

PARASITE

THE TICK SUCKS you out of me in a matter of minutes, but it takes three months before you're born again.

During the waiting period, I scribble down ideas, diagrams, even snippets of dialogue. I fill an entire notebook with jagged letters and little holes where my pencils puncture the paper.

Finally, I'm standing over the tick, biting my fingernails, watching him push the embryonic sack out his tiny ass.

"Does that hurt?" I say.

"Yeah, a little," the tick says. "But it's worth the $500."

"What do you need with $500 anyway?"

"What do you need with a little man?"

You emerge, and cut your way out of the sack, coated with green pus.

"Where did he get the knife?" I say.

"It must be made of calcium deposits," the tick says.

You're still disoriented, swinging at the air, shouting something about the army. I stick you in the black bag.

At dinner, my wife tells me about some non-profit organization, and I pretend to care. She ends up crying—I'm not sure why. Maybe I laughed when I should've frowned.

Later that night, I'm inside the garage, looking into the gerbil cage. The black bag isn't moving, and I'm terrified you're dead.

But then, when I dump you out, you get up and yell, "What the fuck did you do?"

"This isn't about me anymore," I say. Well, recite. "You always made everything about me, but it was always about you. Now you're gonna pay for what you did to me. And mom."

You point your knife at me. "Let me go, or I'm gonna fucking kill you."

I laugh. I laugh at your stupid little knife and your stupid little voice. I used to be so afraid of those eyes, but now they're mine to play with.

So I open my notebook. "You can forget begging for mercy. I have to do this."

"You could've let me stay dead," you say.

You're right, of course. I shouldn't be here right now. I should be in bed, holding my wife in my arms, dreaming this nightmare instead of living it.

But it's too late now.

I reach for the ant farm.

A LONG METAL SIGH

It's Jordon's turn to feed Aunt Laura while she strokes his face with the furry nubs at the end of her arms, but he's dead. And not the kind of dead that keeps you guessing. No, "Is he chatting up Benjamin Franklin in a golden café in the sky?" No, "Will he visit me in my dreams and haunt me with cryptic messages that will ultimately save my life?" This is the kind of dead you can't take back.

A ten year old boy struck him in the back of the head at my nephew's birthday party. Candy didn't erupt from the wound. The birthday clown offered to perform CPR, but when no one said anything, he walked into the house and closed the door.

The parents of the boy told their son that Jordon moved to Africa. So says my father. He also insists that the parents said, "Lies are cheaper than therapy." My father laughs when he tells me this, disgusted, angry.

I say, let the boy live with a song in his heart for a few more years, though I don't say this out loud.

Anyway, I would feed Aunt Laura myself, but I'm being held hostage by a very small man with a very small pistol and mustache.

Like you, I doubted the significance of this weapon. That is, until the demonstration on my pet chinchilla.

I hold the bleeding ball of fuzz in my arms. He's so new that he doesn't have a name yet, but I feel a part of me evaporating, drifting and funneling into the little man.

I want to kill him, the way I'd kill the boy if he were a monster. Not so monstrous that I wouldn't recognize the human in him.

Just monstrous enough.

The chinchilla kicks and startles me. I drop him.

"He's still alive," I say.

"Kill him then," the tiny man says. "I'm not wasting any more bullets."

I scoot the chinchilla under my bed. On the way, I name him Franklin.

"Bring out the photographs," the little man says.

"What photographs?"

"Family photographs! What do you think?" He paces back and forth on the dresser. For the first time, or maybe the second time and I forgot, I notice the man's lack of reflection in the mirror behind him.

I almost ask him if he's a vampire. However, I'm too busy pissing myself and saying, "I don't think I have any photographs."

"Everyone has photographs!" he says, and scratches at his mustache.

My Aunt Laura waddles in. She says, "Would you be a dear and feed me my stuffing?"

The little man points his gun at her. "What the hell is that?"

"She's my aunt," I say. What I don't say is that she's also a teddy bear. Or at least as close to a teddy bear a person could possible be, with hair transplants, amputations, and a mad swarm of cosmetic surgeries. Not to mention two dead parents and a substantial inheritance.

"Please let her go," I say. "She's harmless."

"She's not going anywhere," the man says. "She could call the police."

"She doesn't have hands."

"How do I know she doesn't have a specially made phone she can use?"

"She doesn't."

"So says the guy with the gun pointed at his family. Where are those photographs?" He aims the gun at my face. "Get on it! Now!"

"Who's your little friend?" my aunt says. She fiddles with the perky ears of living flesh attached to the top of her head and steps closer to him. "You look just like a little doll."

"Stay back," the man says.

"Why don't you sit on my bed for a while?" I say. "I need to do something, then we can go eat dinner."

Or maybe I'm not saying this. Maybe I'm not brave enough to say a few damn words, and I watch as my aunt holds out her hands to pick up the little man and press him against her hairy chest.

Before she can lay a hand on him, he shoots her. The miniscule pellet whizzes past the layer of brown fur which cost her more than a bullet proof vest.

She wanted to be lovable. Cuddly. She wanted to light up the faces of children when she entered a room.

Maybe three weeks before he died, Jordon told me over a couple bowls of steaming chili that he was thinking about quitting the caretaking job. He told me that he cried for Aunt Laura almost every night. He said people hugged her less than they used to, before the transformation. We finished the chili.

After this conversation, Jordon didn't make an effort to hug her more often.

Neither did I.

I think about rolling Aunt Laura under my bed with the teddy bear I outgrew but never threw away.

When she opens her mouth, I think she's going to tell me the meaning of life. Blood gushes out instead.

I open another drawer and toss out the innards.

"For god's sake," the man says. "They're in the chest!"

So I open the chest, and find the photographs.

"Here," I say, and hold out the cluster of memories.

"I don't want them," the man says, and I think I detect a hint of sorrow in his voice. A sour sort of sorrow.

"I want you to eat them," he says.

"Eat them or die," he says with the gun.

I eat them. At first they taste sweet, then bitter, then they're gone.

"Now the birthday cards," the man says.

"I don't know where—"

"They're in a tin box under your bed."

I find them. I also find Franklin snuggled up against my old teddy bear.

I start with a birthday card from my grandma with flowers on the cover. Flowers that look nothing like the flowers at Jordon's funeral, but doesn't seem to matter. I remember anyway.

Then I take the wet wad of card out of my mouth. "You do want me to eat these, right?"

"Obviously," the man says, looking smaller all of a sudden.

It goes on like this. He commands me and I obey. I eat letters and gifts and even my teddy bear. Aunt Laura would have tried to talk me out of it if she wasn't so dead.

I dissect my room, devouring all the vital organs. I feel sick to my stomach, the way I felt at the birthday party right after I laughed. I laughed because I knew Jordon couldn't die. I laughed because I already imagined us laughing about it over a couple steaming bowls of chili.

"I need to shit," I say.

"Not yet," the little man says. "You've got to eat me first."

"I don't want to."

He waves the gun. "It's either you or me."

I hold him by the arm and lift him in front of my face. After all this, I guess I expect him to be happy. Instead, he looks as afraid as I feel.

His mustache falls off. Without it, he sort of looks like me.

I can't say that I'm surprised, but I pretend that I am, for my own benefit.

I lift him higher and he says, "Damn it!"

"What?" I say.

"I dislocated my shoulder. Never mind. Hurry up and do it."

So I do.

As his brittle bones snap and crunch in my mouth and his sweet blood oozes down my throat, I feel like a monster. Not so monstrous that I don't recognize the human in me.

Just monstrous enough.

As for the gun, I forgot all about it, and it pops in my mouth, blowing out not one of my teeth.

Still, it's my turn to die. And not the kind that keeps you guessing.

The kind you can't take back.

It's cheaper than therapy.

CAMP

MY MUSCLES TIGHTEN. My teeth clench. My irritable bowel is seriously pissed off.

I'm no good at sitting.

"Hold it together," my dad tells me. Not physically here, of course, but why would that stop him? Hold it together—that's easy for him to say. He's made of steel bars and rivets and bolts. Me, I'm held together with Elmer's glue and pushpins and chewing gum.

Memories vibrate. They fall and crack open.

A few years ago I shit my pants on this very same two and a half hour bus ride. With liquid crap trickling down my legs, I stumbled toward the bus driver. In tears. In shame.

I begged him to take me home, but he said, "Sit down!"

I told him that I was sick, and he laughed at me and said, "No kidding," but I won't shit my pants this time. Even if I do, I'll handle it. I'm bigger and stronger and smarter than I used to be. My dad made sure of that.

Another memory falls off the shelf and smashes on the floor. My first memory.

In this one, I watch my neighbor's pet rabbit kick frantically inside a blender until its legs are too mangled to even tremble anymore.

"This game sucks," Nigel says, beside me, tapping at his phone/camera/mp3 player/game console/everything else.

"Can I play for a while?" I say.

"It doesn't suck that much."

I've never seen or spoken with Nigel outside of Camp and the bus ride to and from, but I still consider him one of my best friends. Mainly because I don't have all that many.

Nigel's a troublemaker and sort of a jerk, and that's why I like him.

"You know, they're going to confiscate that," I say.

"Not unless I keep it in my ass," he says. "They won't check my ass. Not without probable cause anyway."

"That's sick. Would you really do that?"

"You'd have to help me."

"You're sick."

"No kidding."

Once again I'm stuck in the top bunk, despite the fact that I called bottom the moment Nigel and I entered the cabin. I remind him that last year I fell off the top bunk during a night terror and suffered a mild concussion. I also remind him that he promised me on the life of Katherine the Great, his pet Chihuahua, that this year I could have the bottom.

"She died two months ago," he says. That's that.

Hamilton enters the cabin, dressed in yellow and grinning like an idiot as usual. "Hello, boys. Excited about the fire tonight?"

"Yeah," we say, Nigel and I.

"Good."

I shudder.

I don't hate the guy, but sometimes when he's talking I want to punch him in the kidneys.

"Your cell phone please, Nigel," Hamilton says, his hand out and flat like a bear-trap ready to bite. Although mousetrap might be more appropriate. This is Hamilton, after all.

Nigel mumbles something that sounds like, "Poop hound," and hands over the phone.

"I'm not trying to be a dark cloud at a picnic," Hamilton says. "I just want to start our camping experience out right. We're not only here for fun and games. We're also trying to learn some responsibility. And that means following the rules." He sits on the bed and wraps his arm around Nigel's shoulders. "You might not appreciate it now, but someday you will. You won't always have Counselors or parents to bring you what you want. Someday you're going to have to fulfill your own needs, and that's not always an easy thing to do. It's better to start preparing now. Do you understand?"

"Yes," Nigel says. "Please get your hands off me."

Hamilton sighs and heads for the door. "See you at the fire, boys." He smiles and leaves.

For those campers who don't like eating sheep meat, the Counselors supply us with baby back ribs. I watch the sheep spinning on the spit. It reminds me of my neighbor's bunny, turning around and around, staring so intently at nothing.

"Does anyone else have a ghost story?" Kent says, another Counselor.

Nigel raises his hand.

"Go ahead, Nigel."

Nigel stands, though no one else did when they were telling stories. "Years ago, there was a boy murdered at this camp," he says.

A few kids laugh.

"He was a good boy," Nigel says. "He never did any wrong to anybody, so he went to Heaven. The first thing he wanted to do when he got there was meet God. He had all sorts of questions for God about the meaning of life and stuff like that. Mostly, he just wanted to thank God for creating the world. The problem was that a lot of people wanted to meet God, so the line was really, really long. So the boy waited. For years and years. He had a long time to think about what happened to him. He was killed before he ever had the chance to drive a car or fuck a girl or—"

"Nigel, don't be vulgar," Hamilton says, smiling.

"Sorry," Nigel says. "Anyway, the more he thought about it, the angrier he got. By the time he reached the front of the line, his whole body was covered with fire. He didn't care about the meaning of life and he didn't feel like thanking God for anything. All he cared about was getting revenge. God loved the boy and so he sent him back here, to this Camp, like the boy wanted. The reason why I know this is because he talked to me last night in my dreams. He told me to warn all of you to beg for forgiveness. He's not only after the one who killed him, but everyone who didn't stop this terrible thing from happening. Everyone."

There's some laughter, but mostly there isn't.

"He's telling the truth," Mike says. She's one of the few girls who comes to Arthur's Science Camp every year. "I saw the boy last night too," she says. "He asked me to fuck him, but I'm not a whore."

"You can't fuck a ghost," England says, in that stupid fake accent of his.

"Does anyone else have a story?" Hamilton says.

"He's watching us right now," Nigel says. "If you don't apologize, he's going to—"

"Your turn is over, Nigel," Kent says. "Please sit down."

Nigel obeys.

The boy holds hands with the Holy Light and points at me. The Light glares at me in a way that reminds me of my father.

"It wasn't me," I say. "I didn't do it."

The Light comes at me with a belt.

I wake up when I hit the floor.

Luckily, I don't hit my head this time.

A boy rushes into the cabin and I kick at him, even though he's quite a distance away from me.

"Wake up. You have to see this," the boy says, not a ghost, but England. He tugs at the stupid fake necklace of teeth he wears all the time. He always plays with that thing when he's excited.

"What's going on?" Nigel says.

"Come on," England says. "Before they take it away."

So we follow him outside, past the other cabins, toward the Barn. Already, there's a small group of kids standing around the outside of the Barn.

We enter the circle and see the body.

"Shit," Nigel says. "Is it anyone we know?"

"No, it's just some guy," a younger kid says. I don't know his name. He's new.

Tiny spotlights stroke the man's carcass up and down. A flashlight rests for a while pointed at the man's face, and I notice that someone's crapped in his gaping mouth.

"Maybe the ghost did it," England says. "What's his name, Nigel?"

"He forgot his name," Nigel says. "He's too consumed with rage to remember."

Hamilton squeezes through the child barrier, wearing urine-colored pajamas covered with smirking bees. Kent, in his nightgown, is close behind.

"Go back to bed, children," Hamilton says.

No one moves.

"Does anyone know this man?" Kent says, kneeling, searching through pockets.

"He thinks I'm a slut," Mike says.

"No I don't," Kent says.

"Not you, Kent. The dead man."

"Oh."

"Go back to bed, children," Hamilton says. "Or none of us will be allowed in the Barn tomorrow."

Most everyone groans.

"Now," Hamilton says.

We go back to bed.

I'm usually no good at falling asleep, but the instant I hit the mattress, I sleep like a rotting baby.

One swipe of Hamilton's keycard and the Barn door will open, and we can all do what we're here for.

But Hamilton doesn't swipe the keycard. He stands there, staring at us, smiling.

"As I'm sure you all already know, a certain troubling incident took place last night, and we need to talk about it," Hamilton says. "Kent and I haven't been able to ascertain the identity of the man, but we believe he was homeless and living in the woods."

"Then he wasn't homeless," Nigel says. "If he was living in the woods, then the woods was his home."

Hamilton's smile grows a little—which doesn't mean that he's any happier, by the way. "OK, Nigel," Hamilton says. "The point is that we're probably not going to cancel Camp because of what happened, but that doesn't mean we can just forget about it."

Cold wads of water begin to pelt me from above.

"Can we talk about this inside?" England says.

"No one's going into the Barn until we finish this conversation," Kent says.

"He was just some homeless guy," England says. "It's not like he was one of us. Who cares?"

"We should all care," Hamilton says. "Your parents sent you here because they want you to care."

"I'm too fucking cold and wet to care," England says.

"You'd better start," Kent says. "Or you're not going to last very long."

"OK," England says. "Sorry."

Sometimes the other kids put England and Nigel in the same category, but England really isn't much of a rebel. He only talks back because he likes the attention. 99.9% of the time, he doesn't mean what he says.

"The rules and regulations that we follow here don't exist to make our lives more difficult," Hamilton says. "They're here to protect us. To help shape us into very fine young people."

"Not into prostitutes," Mike says.

"That's true," Hamilton says. "But what we're discussing right now is the deceased homeless man."

The dead man floats around like a ghost inside my mind, so I close my eyes to get a better look. I see him so clearly, it startles me. He looks a little like my father.

Hamilton continues, "For safety reasons, we're only allowed to slaughter sheep inside the Barn. We all know that. However, breaking that rule isn't what has Kent and I so concerned. We at Arthur's Science Camp believe that to slaughter an adult not only shows disrespect to us, but to the other authority figures in your lives. I'm talking about your parents. Do you want to disrespect your parents?"

There are a few no's. Most everyone's silent.

"Slaughtering a fully-grown sheep is a privilege at your age," Hamilton says. "Not a right. Only your parent mentor can decide whether or not you've earned that privilege. Not me, not Kent, not any of you. Do you understand?"

"Yes," we say.

He swipes the card.

Nigel leans in close to me and says, "Let's go swimming."

"We can't," I say. "We have to go inside now."

"Suit yourself." He walks away.

So I go in alone, with everyone else.

The young sheep girl squirms and gags, and that's about all she can manage. At some point she'll probably pee her jeans.

My station today is equipped with needles and an axe. Mainly I'll be working with the needles, because the axe is just to finish.

I have thirty minutes before Kent shows up to inspect my work, and my stomach is killing me. I feel like throwing up and shitting at the same time. I feel like exploding.

I start off scratching her skin with a needle tip. In general the skin nearer to the bone is more sensitive than areas with more fatty tissue, so I go for the skin nearer to the bone.

She's trying to talk to me. If she weren't gagged, she'd probably beg for mercy and then when I don't give her any, she'd tell me that she hates me. She'd tell me that I'm going to burn in hell.

I stick a needle in her eye.

She screams silently.

What she doesn't understand is that I'm not doing this because I want to. I don't want to cause her as much pain as humanly possible. This is about need.

I'm going to do a great job, and then I'm going to get my needle badge, and then I'm going to show it to my father. He's going to hold me and tell me that he's proud of me.

I need this badge.

Once again I dream of falling, and I wake up on the floor.

"Come on, guys," England says, without his usual fake accent. "Hurry up."

"Who died this time?" Nigel says.

England doesn't answer.

We follow him to the fire pit.

Hamilton isn't smiling anymore.

I throw up on England. He doesn't care.

Hamilton dangles there, naked, skewered by the sheep spit. But he's not a sheep. He's one of us.

Mike wraps a leaf around Hamilton's small penis, and holds it on with one of her hair bands. "That's better."

"Go to your rooms!" Kent says, rushing in front of Hamilton. He waves at us with a machete. "Go to your rooms now!"

That's what we do.

I sit down next to Nigel on the bottom bunk. My muscles loosen. My teeth relax. My stomach doesn't say a word.

"I can't believe he's gone," I say. "He was annoying, but he didn't deserve this."

"The others we cooked on that fire didn't deserve it either," Nigel says.

"No one deserves it."

"That's different though," I say. "They're only sheep. Hamilton was a wolf like us."

"So we have the right to torture and kill anyone who isn't like us?"

"Not the right, really. It's just the way things are. The world is really overpopulated, and we're a natural defense mechanism."

"Is that what your dad tells you?"

"Well...yeah, but I believe it." My gut's starting to churn again.

"My dad says that every person we kill did something really terrible in a past life. He calls us knights of karmic justice. Everyone's got their reasons, but reasons aren't good enough."

I'm silent for a few moments, as a little spotlight shines inside my brain. "Nigel...did you—"

"Did I kill Hamilton?" He shakes his head. "I haven't killed anyone since I got here, and I'm not planning to."

All I can think to say is, "You're going to get in trouble."

So I do.

Kent dragged me across the camp by the arm, and that's why I'm wet and muddy. He also told me, "Hamilton was like a brother to me. He helped me kill my parents. Do you know what kind of bond that sort of thing creates?" That's why I pissed and shit my pajama pants.

He's standing over me with a bloody machete, breathing hard. I notice his trophies on the nearby shelf. Scalps and dried ears mostly.

"Did you do it?" Kent says.

I shake my head.

He kneels on top of my legs and presses the blade against my forehead. "Mike says she saw you sneaking outside her cabin, heading right towards Hamilton's place."

"That's not true," I say, shitting my pants even more. "Mike's a liar. Everyone knows that."

"Yeah, and that's why I haven't sliced your fucking neck open already."

He stands. "Then again, she might be telling the truth this time. How do I know?"

"I didn't do it," I say.

"Not just anyone could take out Hamilton. He was a monster. But you. You're better than most of the others here. You could have done it."

I can't help but smile.

He stares down at me and shakes his head. "Go back to your room. I need to think."

On my way out I hear muffled cries coming from his closet. Probably two children, a boy and a girl. I know how Kent thinks.

There's no denying it. That's Hamilton's keycard in Nigel's hand.

"You killed him," I say.

"I'm not like that anymore," Nigel says. "I found this in the mud."

"You killed Hamilton so you could free those stupid sheep."

"I am going to free them, but I didn't kill anyone."

"Kent's going to kill me because of you!" I race forward and trip on the mud before I can touch Nigel.

"I didn't do it," Nigel says, and heads for the Barn.

"Help!" I say, louder than I've ever been in my whole life. No one leaves their cabins. Not even England. As far as they know, Kent's murdering me, and they don't want any part of that. I don't blame them.

I do, however, blame Nigel.

So I follow him into the Barn.

Nigel's already in the cage, snipping cable ties with a wire cutter.

"If they hear you crying, they'll come in and kill us," Nigel says.

The children only cry harder.

"Fuck," Nigel says.

I stand there, watching him for a while. He looks so full of himself. So happy. But he's not the great guy that he thinks he is. He's going to get everyone killed. All the campers, Kent, our parents. Me.

And for what? A few stupid sheep who're already too traumatized to be worth anything to society.

I pick up a finishing gun from a nearby table and make sure it's loaded. It is. I cock it.

"You have to run away as fast as you can," Nigel says. "Keep running until you can't run anymore. Then hide. The people who find you will take you to your moms and dads." Nigel's looking right at me and the gun as he's saying all this.

I lift the gun.

Would I really kill one of my best friends?

Well, maybe I'm possessed by the spirit of the ghost kid. Maybe Nigel's the one who killed him years ago and this is his final revenge.

What I know for sure is that I don't want to kill Nigel.

I need to.

Reasons are good enough.

I aim and fire.

I fire again at one of the sheep who's running right at me, or the door, I'm not sure which. I hit him in the neck. I must have hit the carotid artery because he's gushing.

Most of the sheep run away. Some don't.

I walk over to Nigel.

He's saying, "Hello kitty. Hello kitty. Hello kitty," with a bullet hole in his head.

I don't think he's ever even owned a cat.

My muscles tighten. My teeth clench. I feel like shitting and pissing and throwing up, but there's nothing left inside me.

I'm no good at being strapped down on a cold metal table, waiting for the inevitable.

"We have to get out of here," I say. "Nigel let the sheep go. They'll find help and the cops will come after us."

"No," Kent says. "The sheep won't make it. The Camp is located here for a reason."

"I...I didn't kill Hamilton. It was Nigel. I had to—"

"No. Mike killed Hamilton. England saw the whole thing. He agreed to tell me who did it if he could slaughter the culprit himself. I agreed. She's next."

I wondered who was in the bag he carried in. It must be her.

I picture England sliding his hunting knife across Mike's stomach and all the campers gasping. England will love it.

Whether or not Mike actually killed Hamilton is anyone's guess.

This can't be happening to me.

"If you kill me, my dad will eat you alive," I say. I want to scream the words, but I'm almost whispering.

"Your dad won't do shit," Kent says. "I know him. He cares a lot more about himself than he does about you. If he ate me, every parent mentor of every kid here would be after him. Anyway, your father will expect me to kill you. You broke the most important rule. You killed Nigel."

"But..."

Kent gags me before I can say anything more. It doesn't really matter. I'd probably just beg for mercy and then when I don't get any, I'd tell him that I hate him. I'd tell him that he's going to burn in hell.

Maybe I do tend to kill adults while I'm sleepwalking and dreaming of slaughtering my father. That doesn't mean I did anything wrong.

Kent blasts me with his nail gun.

Most of the kids gasp. Some laugh. And that hurts more than the nail.

Kent's not doing this because he wants to. He doesn't want to cause me as much pain as humanly possible. This is about need.

I'm going to be an example that no one will ever forget.

This is all Nigel's fault.

AMERICAN SHEEP

One moment you're prepping your flesh-stick for a heaping dose of midget porn, and the next you're lying face up in a room packed with disemboweled sheep while something's sucking on your ass.

Like me, you stand and find you were sitting on the open mouth of a small tube. An air-sucking tube, like you'd find in a mail-room or Costco. These tube-holes wheeze at you from all over the floor, all over the walls, the ceiling. They're color-coded. Numbered. you must be insane.

"Apothegm #223," a voice says. "All inhales must exceed two seconds."

It's a man's voice, coming from the speaker mounted to the wall.

"Apothegm #223 has been transgressed. Liberate the sheep now."

A plastic container shoots out from one of the ceiling tubes, and falls directly into one of the floor tubes.

"Damn it," the man says.

A few moments later the container bursts from the wall. This time it lands safely on some bloody wool.

I've never smelled a room full of dead sheep before, but the scent is too real not to be.

My eyes dart around like I know what I'm doing. Like I have a plan. Maybe one more blink of my leaking eyes and I'll remember I'm actually a secret agent or an alien. Not a website designer with a degree in philosophy who hasn't thought about the meaning of life for over two years.

Or.

Maybe this is hell.

Maybe this is heaven.

Maybe the lion won't play nice when sleeping by the lamb.

What I know is that there aren't any windows. There's a door, but I don't check to see if it's locked. Fuck fight or flight. I feel like standing here in my Spongebob boxers, staring at my hands.

"Liberate the sheep."

For some reason, I think he's telling me to bring them back to life, so I say, "They're dead."

"Liberate the sheep."

His voice is assertive, but soothing. Like the speaker of an audiobook. You don't want the reader's mind to wander, but you don't want to scare anyone away either.

"Where am I?" I mean to say, but I actually say, "Who am I?"

And he says, "Liberate the sheep, Pith."

That's not my name.

"Open up the cartridge," the man says.

I try the door, finally, but it's locked.

"Open up the cartridge." This time it's me talking. I open the blood-smeared plastic container and find knives, saws, scissors, tubes, funnels, and a laminated instruction manual. English on one side. Spanish on the other.

It tells me how to drain the blood. How to cut up the flesh into long, skinny strips. How to saw bone. It tells me which bits go into which holes. It tells me good luck. It tells me to remember my goggles because safety always comes first. It tells me Made in America.

Orange Tube #27 eats the last of the intestines, and I realize that I'm drugged. It's rather obvious to me at this point, because I should be screaming. Not working.

I shouldn't even consider this work.

The decomposing elephant in the room is the fact that the drugs inside me will eventually wear off.

Then where will I be?

I'm afraid that I'll still be here, coated with blood and gut juice, only clear-headed and scared shitless.

My only hope. If you count sheep to fall asleep, maybe you un-count sheep to wake up.

Three, two, one.

The last eyeball rockets away through Blue Tube #3.

I did the eyeballs last, because they made me feel less alone.

"Apothegm #184," the man says. "You must wear knitted sweaters every day except Flag Day."

The only shirt I'm wearing is made of dry blood.

"Apothegm #184 has been transgressed."

A rumbling sound molests my ears. It doesn't get louder, but it sounds angrier. I imagine the tubes blasting me with water. Mountain spring water. Cleaning me.

Cleansing me.

Saving me.

But instead of water, they vomit the sheep back at me. Bones and organ chunks punch me from all sides. Wads of wool pelt me. Strips of flesh slap me. I'm breathing blood.

As a kid, I thought a toilet or a bathtub could whisk me away from my loving home if I wasn't careful. Now, I wish the tubes would take me. I wouldn't mind the sewers. I wouldn't mind the diarrhea rivers or the giant rats or the orphaned alligators. Give me mole people. Give me radioactive mutants. Give me anything, so long as I can understand what the fuck is going on.

"Go to Room 9," the man says. "Not an Apothegm. Just some friendly advice."

Outside, I'm in a hallway with art on the walls.

Paintings. At a time like this.

I want to burn them all.

Part of me wants to make a run for it.

Part of me knows that when the man said, "Just some friendly advice," he really meant, "Do it or you're dead."

It's surprising how perceptive you can be when your world's turned upside-down and inside-out.

No, my world's a fucking Mad Lib.

I wake up to a room filled with (adjective) (noun).

Disemboweled sheep.

Inside Room 9 there are (adjective) (noun).

Cannibalistic clowns.

But no, inside Room 9, there are actually dead bodies. They're each lying on their own bed. Some more decayed than others.

I vomit and scream at the same time, and it's a messy combination.

"There's a small device planted somewhere in your body," the man says. "Try to enter Room 1, and you'll die. Room 1 is the only way out."

"Fuck you!" I say, because there's nothing else to do.

"Apothegm #42. All words beginning with the letter F must not be spoken aloud. Apothegm #42 has been transgressed."

Now it's time to (verb) the (noun.)

I don't want to eat the soup.

The air smells too much like death, and the taste of the soup somehow overwhelms the stench of the air, but the door closed and locked behind me and I can't get out. The soup is almost black. It has no texture. It tastes runny. What it ran out of, I don't want to imagine. Though I do.

To make the soup, I imagine you dump the worst things you can imagine into a blender. Then you do research to find more obscure horrible things, and add those to the concoction as well. Then you let the blender run for three days straight.

"Eat the soup, Pith."

I don't want to eat the soup.

Suddenly, or maybe not so suddenly, depending on how long I've been holding my spoon, music erupts around me.

Patriotic music. At a time like this.

I want to snuff out the entire orchestra.

America the Beautiful.

God Bless America.

This Land is Your Land.

The National Anthem.

The National Anthem again.

I notice that it's in alphabetical order.

I notice that I've spewed the dark fluid back into my bowl.

I notice that it hasn't stopped me from doing my job.

Apothegm #398. You must not blink more than 10 times per minute.

The soup starts out as a punishment.

Now it's a reward.

Now I flatten dead chickens with a mallet for a bowl of that black ooze.

Apothegm #1077. You must not bend your elbows from 5AM to 9PM.

Days pass.

Weeks.

When I think the word months, I start to cry.

Apothegm #75. You must not have a spleen.

The only reason I do the jobs is so that the door will open. So that I can go to another room and do a different job. Sometimes the new job is better. Sometimes worse. It doesn't matter.

There are moments of crippling terror, but most of the time I feel numb.

Apothegm #218. You must be of European descent at all times.

I work because the jobs are there to be done.

I eat the soup because it's there to be eaten.

I talk to the man because he talks back.

I'm only alive because I'm not dead.

My routine shatters when I enter Room 12.

"Sit down," the man says. "Join me."

It's him, sitting at a table topped with a cluster of gourmet foods and fine china and unlit candles. The table legs are shaped like dolphins.

They're swimming. At a time like this.

I don't want to hurt them. I love animals.

"You," I say. A very sick part of me is happy to see him. "What are you doing here?"

"I'm trying to have dinner with you." He toasts at me with his wine glass.

For the first time I notice the leash he's holding with his other hand. I notice the dog by his side. Not a pit bull, but a friendly-looking dog, like the man himself.

"We're having veal parmesan," the man says. "No soup." He laughs.

So do I. The sound makes me want to stick a fork in my neck.

And then, it hits me like a kick in the balls. I know this guy. At first, I'm sure he's a second cousin. Then, I remember.

"You're that Senator," I say. "You're supposed to be in jail."

"You're supposed to be at the movies with your girlfriend."

"I don't have one. You're supposed to be in jail."

"Let's not repeat ourselves."

This is him. That corrupt asshole who committed treason after treason, and now he's sitting there in his fucking suit, staring at me.

Somehow, I feel betrayed. I thought I was dealing with an ordinary psychopath. But this guy, he fucks over billions of people in his sleep.

I thought I was special.

"I imagined you shorter," the Senator says. "Fatter. They told me you work on computers."

"With computers." This is my rebellion. Pathetic.

In a horrible instant, I realize what he was implying by "imagined." He's never seen me before. There are no cameras in the hallway or the rooms.

What he's telling me is that he doesn't need to watch me. He presses his buttons. Flips his switches. He gets off on knowing that he doesn't have to see my obedience, because he has full confidence that I'll do as I'm told.

And he's right.

"You might find this hard to believe," he says, after swallowing. "But you're my retirement gift."

My body lurches forward at a speed that surprises me. I feel like my skin would split open and my bones would come spilling out if I tried to stop now.

The dog gallops at me. In a moment, I'm sure he'll chomp on my crotch. Instead, I kick him hard in the face. The Senator laughs. Giggles.

I turn around and watch him exit the room. I watch the door close and I hear the lock lock.

All night, or at least what I decide is night due to the lack of work, the dog lies on the floor, trembling, whimpering.

I sit at the table, but I don't feel like eating.

Someone in some philosophy book somewhere once said that expectations are a bitch. Not in those words exactly, but you get the idea. If you don't expect things to get any better, then even the worst situations can feel tolerable.

Stop believing in heroes, and you won't feel like such a victim.

Forget the police, forget the FBI. Forget your family. Your friends. Forget the comics you've read, and the movies you've seen. You're trapped here. This is your life. Accept it.

And then one day you're busy stuffing a dead cow with light bulbs when the door opens. A girl walks in.

She's wearing a shirt with flowers on it.

Daisies. At a time like this.

I want to kiss her.

"Jesus," she says. "What the fuck is this?"

"You have to get help. I..." There's more to say, obviously, but I'm busy sobbing. Heaving.

"Are you alright?"

"No." I shake my head, as if the act will help me stop crying. It sort of works. "Some sick fuck Senator is keeping me here. I've been here for months." Maybe a year, though I can't stand to say it.

"That sick fuck is my father," she says.

"Oh."

"Let's get out of here."

"I can't. He put something inside me. I don't know what to do."

"I'll get help. Don't worry. I won't let him get away with this."

"Thank you."

"Granola granola."

"What?"

"Granola granola granola granola granola granola."

"What?"

She's out the door. "Granola." It closes behind her.

"Oh fuck," I say. Heaving.

The speaker activates with a staticky cough.

I hear him laughing. Giggling.

You're trapped here.

This is your life.

Accept it.

Years pass.

When I think the word decade, I slap my face.

A day doesn't go by that I don't open the door to Room 1, and look at those stairs that could lead me to liberty above.

Maybe this is heaven.

Maybe this is hell.

Maybe the Senator's heaven is my hell. And maybe when you realize that, the meaning of life doesn't matter anymore. Maybe you can stop thinking and just do your fucking job.

"Apothegm #1," the Senator says. "There was never any device inside you. All you ever had to do was enter Room 1, and you could have left. I would have let you go." He's quiet for a moment, then says, "Go now."

The door opens.

I'm free.

But I don't feel like liberating myself.

I want to go to bed.

INSIDE

THROUGH THE CORNER of my eye, Lucian looks something like a scarecrow with his arms outstretched, crows scratching and nibbling at loose shoulder hay. Head on, he looks more like me five or so hours ago. Only the little machines hacked out chunks of my remaining calf muscle, not my shoulder. I still own my shoulders.

Lucian shivers because he hasn't learned to smile on his own yet.

"Is he cold?" the little girl outside says.

"No, he's fine," her mother says, or her nanny, or whoever's job it is to lie to her at the moment.

I think of mother first since my mother told me at least twice a day that she wasn't going to die, even though the letter I found in the trash said she was a "DEAD BITCH." My mother also told me on numerous occasions that my father was a good man. What she didn't tell me was that he kept sticking his nose in other people's (important people's) business. This was back when he had a nose to speak of.

The smallest of the machines carries the hunk of Lucian in its tiny pincers and deposits the flesh into the open slot.

Lucian waves goodbye, trembling, then the glass darkens.

As soon as the machines release him, he thrashes at them with his good arm and leg. They don't put up a fight. Lucian manages to break off one of the protruding eye sensors from the machine that stuck the needle in the back of his head. He laughs like this is some sort of victory. I don't watch the machines rolling through their mouse hole exits, but I know they are.

"You're going to pay for that," I say.

"With what?" he says, and laughs again.

The answer's obviously pain, because what else could it be here? Still, I don't tell him. If he wants my help, he can stop laughing at me.

Rea takes a break from her throaty mumbling. She says, "You still haven't told us why you're here. What did you do?"

"I didn't do anything," Lucian says.

"Of course you did," she says. "Maybe you don't know what you did, but you did something."

"No. Jesus. You don't understand. I'm not one of you. I have a soul."

Now it's my turn to laugh.

I remember the fields of my childhood because I still own my memories. For now.

For now I remember my father's dirty hands and the way he'd chase after me, declaring himself a zombie farmer each and every time, as if I'd somehow forget the game. I would escape the fields into our home and the moment I stepped through that threshold, I was safe. As soon as the killer zombie walked through the doorway, he was my father again. And my mother, she would call me her Little Dinner Bell. Then we would eat.

Once I spied on my father during one of his secret meetings in the barn. I couldn't hear what he said to those dozen or so people, but the force of his words and gestures frightened me. They wounded me, much more than the slap across the face after he discovered me outside. It wasn't difficult to find me. After the meeting ended, I just sat there by my peephole, shaking and needing to cry.

Later that night, I wandered in the dark, into the fields, and pissed on as many vegetables as I could. I thought about all those people swallowing their meals, the residue of this night invading their bodies. It wouldn't matter how much they washed the greens beforehand. It's never enough.

The next day my father apologized. Then he told me something ridiculous like, "When I slapped you, Terrance, I was really slapping myself." He also told me, "I hate myself for bringing you into this world. You're too good for all this. I'll try to make things better."

Maybe he did. Just not for me.

I remember the fields of my childhood because I don't want to watch the grinning faces outside.

I can't look down to see the machines carving up the nub that was once my left leg, but I know they are. I know the blades excrete a trail of bright green ooze in their wake. I know I won't bleed. And I know that I'll wave goodbye to that piece of me when it leaves, and I'll smile, because I'm supposed to enjoy this.

"I heard something interesting this morning," Rea says.

"Oh yeah, where?" Lucian says. "The news?" He snorts.

"I heard it from some teenagers talking on the street. You can learn a lot about the world if you just listen."

Lucian scoffs a scoff that probably means, "Why should I listen to them if they won't listen to me?"

"Anyway," Rea says. "I heard there's an organization called HARM that's been freeing people like us all over the country. I don't know what HARM stands for."

"So what?" Lucian says. "You think they're going to free us?"

"They probably won't," she says. "I just thought it was interesting. That's all."

"Right."

I hate the way he talks to her. It's as if he doesn't see the power erupting from her eyes. It's as if he's not afraid.

I am. It's the force of her words and gestures. They wound me like a memory.

"It had to be a computer error," Lucian says. "They'll figure it out soon. When they set me free, there'll be hell to pay."

I was freed once.

I was freed from the orphanage with all the other soulless children. You see, God would never kill both parents of a child with a soul. He would never allow real children to live seven to a room. He would never allow the beatings or words like Little Fuckers to violate their ears.

Father Sherman, he blessed me once with his metal switch, and from that point on I decided to do everything right. I decided to eat right, sleep right, walk right, shit right. I decided to be the best Little Fucker I could be.

And so, when I looked at the cuts and bruises and black eyes on the other children, and looked at my own flawless body in the mirror, I almost felt free.

The organization that broke us out weren't called HARM, but ANGEL. I never learned what it stood for. I never asked.

None of the safe houses were safe enough, so I moved around until I couldn't anymore. Until I was stuck.

It didn't matter how much they saved me.

It's never enough.

The three of us stand side by side by side, and Lucian trembles, because he still hasn't learned how to smile right.

I don't watch the teenage boy selecting Rea's breasts on the electronic panel outside, but I know he is. Rea knows too.

The boy comes here every Friday afternoon for the same thing.

I don't own my legs anymore, so one of the machines has to hold me up as I face the glass and spread what's left of my arms and smile like a good Little Fucker.

The machine with the blades carves out another slice of Rea's left breast.

When the machine with the pincers carries the slice away, the glass darkens and we're released.

I use my good arm to pull me to my bench, and Lucian goes on another pointless rampage.

The people outside, they can't see inside right now, but we can see out. We can always see out.

The boy must know this.

He stands by the glass, this time and every other time, and he chews the sliver of Rea. Probably twenty dollars worth. It's small. But it's more than enough to get the job done. You can see it on his face.

Rea doesn't have to watch him, but she does. She watches him, with the eye sensor that Lucian broke off the machine in her one good hand, stroking it, turning it counter-clockwise, murmuring something about treacherous mouths and lying tongues.

"What are you saying?" Lucian says, after the machines go away.

"A psalm," Rea says.

"Great," Lucian says. "I'm sure that's going to save us."

"No one's going to save us."

Lucian approaches Rea, and for a second or two I'm afraid he's going to hurt her. Instead, he collapses on the floor and cries. Through the corner of my eye, he looks something like a scared little boy.

"It doesn't have to be like this," I say. "When the red light goes on, you can stand and hold out your arms yourself and wave when you're supposed to. If you do that, the machine won't have to force you. You don't have to be controlled. And if you smile on your own, they'll take away the pain during the processing. The needles they stick in our heads can do that. Just smile."

It's almost like freedom.

The teenage boy heads home to his family.

"I'll never smile for them," Lucian says, through his tears. "I don't care what they do to me."

"There are reasons to smile," Rea says. "Do you want to know mine?"

Lucian says no by curling up in silence. Head on, he looks like me in the orphanage, years ago. The day I gave up.

"I want to know," I say.

Rea places the eye sensor in her mouth and swallows. "I've cursed my flesh hundreds, maybe thousands of times since I've been here. These are powerful hexes, and anyone who eats me will learn that I'm not a piece of meat. They'll taste the power of my soul."

Lucian rolls on his back and says, "You're a deluded bitch." Then he tells her, "I can tell you're one of them. You have no soul."

"Everyone has a soul," Rea says.

That's why she's here, of course. She told me. She told me that she opened up in a public forum, and told them what she believes. Someone recorded her, sent the recording to the government, and that was enough to get her thrown in here.

Anyone who says that everyone has a soul obviously doesn't have one herself.

"I need to get out of here," Lucian says. "This is a mistake."

I'm scared, but I drag myself over to Rea's bench and sit beside her.

She's whispering sharp words with her hand on what's left of her breast.

Ever since I was a good Little Fucker, I didn't believe in souls. I didn't care what my parents taught me. I thought it didn't matter what I did, because it's never enough. I can't save anything.

But maybe I'm wrong.

So I say, "Can you curse me too?"

She opens her eyes and nods. She places her hand on me, as if I'm more than a piece of meat. She closes her eyes again. She grumbles ancient curses.

I'm shaking and needing to cry. Then I do.

"What about the children?" I say. "Sometimes parents feed us to their children."

"Them too," Rea says. "Everyone who eats us will be affected. This isn't about revenge, Terrence. This is about making things better."

"Will it? Will it be better?"

"Maybe."

Just not for us.

No one will save me, but maybe when I'm gone, I'll still own something that no one can buy.

The red light goes on.

And it's my turn to smile.

THE HOLE

IF YOU HAVEN'T seen a 50,000 ton earthmover lately, look it up online, or stand here with me by the Plasma Shack display window, sucking on your filter, and watch our government blast one of these rabid puppies toward the moon.

"It's wrong," my sister would say. Along with all her nail-biting cohorts around the globe, of course. They have a problem with the fact that the Secretary of Defense once owned the company that's paying for this multi-billion-dollar operation. I say, they're getting the job done, so who gives a shit?

Washington the Earthmover funnels into the Hole, atom by atom. The process will take about three days, but I'm only willing to devote three more minutes.

After about two and a half, crimson sparks gush out of the Hole. For a moment, I'm afraid this is It. The end. But no, it's only static.

Still, this could be the Enemy's work.

Like the girl beside me says, "Fucking Ens."

The Enemy usually sticks to poking at the big fish, like the stock market, government agency networks, and resource distribution super computers. But sometimes, they practice on us. They experiment.

I bet the little Enemies-in-training sit in their air-conditioned classrooms and molest our TV screens, our homes, our lives, and they laugh at us. Then after a blackout or a car crash, they give each other high fives. Or sixes. Whatever.

"Fucking Ens," I say.

And I repeat this phrase, mindlessly, after the clown in a pink tutu pulls a knife on me in the parking lot.

"What did you call me?" he says, and drops the knife.

I could probably kick his head when he bends down to retrieve his weapon, but I don't.

Instead, I say, "Nothing."

"Give me your wallet and your jewelry."

I hand over my wallet. "I don't have any jewelry."

"Your watch."

I'm not sure if that counts as jewelry. I don't say so.

Even now, with hot urine slithering down my leg, I don't blame the clown. He's a victim of the Enemy, just like you and me and everyone we know. If the government didn't have to spend so much on the war, maybe this guy would get a fair piece. Maybe then his smile would be real, instead of two painted on purple slugs.

"I should cut you for calling me a faggot," he says.

"I didn't," I say.

He goes on to say more, and I think I catch the word diatribe, but I'm not really listening at this point. The knife creeps closer.

When he loses his grip again, the weapon doesn't fall to the cement. For a moment, the blade sits in the air. Then it flips. Then it jitters its way to the clown's eye. The contorting metal wiggles inside the flesh, and blood soon replaces the tears painted on the man's cheeks.

You might imagine a sizzling energy spewing from my fingertips or my third eye, and you might imagine my brow furrowed in dense concentration. But that's not how it is.

I'm standing here shuddering in the cold with my forehead baking in fear, and all I'm really thinking about is how I need to get Einstein to his novelty pork chop shaped heat rock.

The clown gurgles.

As soon as I see a message of blood forming on his puffy orange shirt, I know it's time to go. I read, "My father is," before managing to turn around.

Someone will call the police. Not me.

Maybe he'll live.

I slide into my car, and suffice it to say, I'm more than a little surprised.

I haven't done anything like this since I was a kid.

"About half a dozen rankin...rankin...rankin..." my father says.

He says this because of the Enemy. Because if the government didn't have to spend so much on the war, I'm sure a vaccine or something would have been discovered years ago. Maybe then my father could say "raisin."

"They're all on it down half a dozen," my father says.

And if I'm going to be completely honest, sometimes I blame my father.

Maybe if he'd become someone important, instead of a construction worker, he wouldn't be like this. Maybe he would have eaten better and lived in a neighborhood with less poison in the water and the air and everywhere.

Maybe my father could have tried harder.

"It wouldn't kill you to talk to him," Kaelin says. She scrubs at the shit-stain on the ground. The shit itself is wrapped up in a napkin beside her. I wish she would throw it away already.

"He can't understand me," I say.

"You don't know that," she says. She carries the napkin on the palm of her hand, almost like she's about to give someone a present. But she drops it in the trash. The shit is one of the main reasons why my father is confined to his room. That, and the rest of the house isn't dementia-proof. He once cut his arm with a pair of scissors, which he then cooked in the oven alongside his granddaughter's favorite doll. By the end of it, the two objects had melded together into a cyborg of sorts.

"He likes hearing our voices," my sister says. "They're familiar. It's a comfort to him."

"You've always seen things that aren't there, Kaelin," I say.

She sighs.

The smiling faces in the photographs all over the walls stare at me, but don't see anything, as I scoop another mound of mashed potatoes into my father's mouth. Kaelin thinks these images make my father happy. I think she's the one that's happy.

"Would you like Taran to read you a story, Dad?" she says, and plucks the apples out of my father's collection of shoes.

"Everyone down in the reason," my father says. "The reason."

If I could, I would launch my invisible energy into my father's mind, and piece everything back together again.

But I can't.

My power is all about intentions, but in real life, good intentions are never good enough.

My father's already gone.

"The reason," he says. "The reason."

Einstein's right at home with the likes of Charles Darwin, Marvin Harris, Nikola Tesla. He belongs. Aside from my father and my sister, these are about the only other people in my life.

And yes, they are people.

It doesn't matter that they're snakes. They're also great minds, trapped in my cages, eating my mice. I can see beyond their physical forms and sense their past lives, as that's one of my many awesome powers. Or maybe I just pretend that it is. Whatever.

Marie Curie coils and prepares to strike.

"You're safe," I say to the mouse.

I may be lying, because nothing's happening. But at the last possible instant, the mouse shifts into the air. He swims in place.

"You're dead," I say, and he falls.

In a few suffocating moments, my words become reality. I'm so excited, I crap my pants a little bit. I thought the clown ballerina fiasco was a fluke, but this. This means I'm special.

I head to the bathroom to wipe my ass.

Years ago when I attended the Redmount School of Psychokinesis,

I never killed anyone or anything. Mostly, I sat in an air-conditioned classroom, trying to move metal cubes across my desk, while the other kids laughed and gave each other high fives when they succeeded.

If you've never suffered through a psychokinesis school, you probably think it's a lot of fun. But the constant surveillance isn't fun. The Protocol isn't fun. And fuck if Solitary's ever any fun.

Sitting here on the toilet, moving a ceramic iguana back and forth across my sink, I remember crying alone in that plain white room. I remember my teacher saying, "I know you didn't break Protocol on purpose. But this is the way it has to be or you'll never learn," before she slammed and bolted the door.

That's the worst part. It's your subconscious that performs the psychokinesis. Not you. But you're always punished along with it anyway.

I didn't want to trip anyone or fling food or stab Marty Martinez the Student Body President with a pencil. I didn't intend to be a bully. Sure, part of me hated everyone for doing what I couldn't, but every time I was set free from that plain white room, I almost cried happy stupid tears when I saw my classmates again.

"I'm trying," I told my dad on the phone. Long distance. "My mind just won't listen to me."

"Try harder," he told me.

Like usual, I begged him to take me home.

Like usual, he said no.

He wanted me to be important, and I hated him for it. Every time I cried in the plain white room, wishing for smiling faces instead of plain whiteness, I hated him for not saving me.

I return to my snakes, and a thought comes to me like Godzilla comes to Tokyo. I know I can't win, but I fight anyway. With everything I have.

In the end, I'm sitting on the cold floor, staring at my hands, thinking my monster thought.

I can't save my father. I don't have the power. But I can do the second best thing.

And get my revenge.

"You can't," my sister says, and for once she stops working. She was busy transferring diapers from one large box to another large box. Now she's not. "No one who enters the Hole ever comes back. There might not be a way back."

"I'm not going there to come back, Kaelin," I say. "I'm going to fight the fucking Ens."

"You don't even know what they're capable of."

"I don't care. Life is a constant battle because of them. They shoot their rays and their emissions across the Universe and fuck with us without ever stepping foot on our planet. They make me sick."

"It's galaxies away, Taran. That's too far."

"Sooner or later, they'll find a way to break through our shields and firewalls and armor. If that happens, civilization will collapse in a second. I can't twiddle my thumbs and do nothing."

"Dad needs you."

"No."

"I need you, Taran."

"You know that's not true."

She sits in silence. Not because she's given up on stopping me. She just knows that I'm immature and rebellious, and listing reasons for me to stay will only make me want to run away more.

"I'm going now," I say.

"You mean going going?" she says.

"Yes."

Tears trickle down her cheeks. She hugs me and squeezes me and it hurts.

"You can't do this," she says.

"Goodbye, Kaelin."

"At least say goodbye to him."

"No," I say.

My father snores.

Somewhere between the Earth and the moon, I funnel into the Hole, atom by atom, along with the other Space Force recruits. I think about my snakes. I wonder if they'll enjoy freedom in the wild, or just die trying.

The three days are almost up, and no one's said much of anything. I don't mind.

I'm not afraid, because if I ask my subconscious to protect me from a giant blob or a swarm of alien insects or whatever the fucking Ens are, it will obey me. I will be saved.

The Enemy created the Hole so they could spit their venom onto our world, but the Hole will be their undoing.

I'm coiled and ready to go.

Lights flash.

I can't breathe.

The moon disappears.

When I open my eyes, I expect to find a battlefield raging on outside the window.

I see thousands of missiles and ships and tanks and jeeps. I see geodesic domes. I see Washington the Earthmover.

They're all floating in a chaotic and inactive heap.

There's not a planet or an Enemy in sight.

A nearby ship hails us with a beep. It's my job to activate the intercom, so I do.

"Welcome to the Junkyard," the man says from the other ship.

I deactivate the intercom.

So maybe the Enemy aren't here. And maybe they're not anywhere.

Like the girl beside me says, "They're not fucking real."

What I know for sure is that I didn't run away to escape nothing.

I left everything behind.

I didn't see the whole message written with the clown's blood, but I know what it said. It said, "My father is still in there."

TROUT

ONCE AGAIN, AT exactly 10:43, the trout wriggle their way from the black holes of the polka dot wallpaper, and I'm still not in love.

Maggie screams.

The fish whiz from one side of the room to the other, slapping me with their wet tails, knocking over not a few of my antique lamps onto the pillow mounds I set up on the carpet.

One fish slaps me especially hard in the face, and I catch him. I'm not surprised to find that it's Shard, my least favorite trout of all time.

"What's wrong with her?" I say, squeezing him.

"There's nothing wrong," Shard says. "This isn't about wrong. Didn't we already talk about this? A million times?"

"She has a doctorate, Shard. Don't you, Maggie?"

A very pale Maggie nods in silence.

"Does that mean nothing to you?" I say to the fish.

"Not really," Shard says. "I mean, that's quite an accomplishment, but it doesn't make any difference to us."

"I should just paint over your holes and be done with this nonsense."

"You can't get rid of us that easily."

"I'll use lead-based paint."

"I know I said I believed you," Maggie says, very quiet. "But I didn't. I thought you were crazy."

"And you still wanted to be with me?" I say.

"Yeah."

I don't tell her how stupid that sounds.

"Why do you think they always come at 10:43?" Maggie says.

"Ask him," I say, holding out the trout.

"Well?" Maggie says.

"It's sort of a big secret," Shard says. "It's connected with the meaning of the Universe. If I told you, there would be dire consequences. Do you still want to know?"

She nods.

Shard wiggles free of my grip, and whispers the secret in her ear. Then her flesh erupts from her soul, blinding me with blood, and I wipe my eyes clean in time to see her light funnel into one of the black polka dots.

"Why would she do that?" I say.

"You're never going to love anybody until you start trying to understand them," Shard says.

I grumble, and don't tell him how stupid that sounds.

Maybe next time I'll try a lawyer.

SIN EARTH

FINDING A PYRAMID of sticky bluebursts and a bucket of water before your doorway doesn't necessarily mean that the villagers of Sin Earth respect you, or even like you. The act may instead imply that no one really wants to see your face outside as they're living what my mother would call their pathetic little lives, singing and dancing and eating and sometimes carving ancient faces from spirewood that they burn right after, because otherwise the Enforcers would beat the culprits senseless with sacred clubs.

One such club rots away under the table where I set my bluebursts. Enforcer Yor gave me this weapon the day of my mother's funeral. "She was a good woman," he told me. "Very reliable." Then he handed me his club, which he described in almost the same way.

I pluck the top fruit off the pyramid, and chew. Juicy, delicious. But my mother still says, "You deserve better than this animal food." She says, "Go to the barracks and ask for a decent meal. They'll take care of you."

I take another bite. "I'd rather stay in my hut today."

Every day.

"Well," she says. "At least you'll avoid the rabble."

Don't get me wrong. I don't particularly enjoy staying cooped up in my room, my mother haunting me with wispy words, unable to let go. But usually, I'd rather stay in here, than go out there.

At least here I don't feel a hundred eyes peeling off my flesh, draining my blood, staring at that festering blotch I can't wash off or shit out.

Here, at least I can pretend.

A crow dives through my window and lands on my mother's chair and nibbles at a string on his leg. I untie the note.

"What are you reading?" my mother says. She would examine the letter herself, of course, but I'm the only thing she can see anymore.

"It's from the Thundershines," I say.

"Those fools never wrote me any letters. What do they want?"

"They're inviting me for tea."

She laughs.

The crow nudges at one of the bluebursts with his beak.

"Go ahead," I say.

So the crow pecks away.

"Go ahead what?" my mother says.

"I was talking to the crow."

"Never mind the beast. You write a letter to Grandma Thundershine and thank her for the offer but tell her you'd much rather devour your own legs." She chuckles.

"I don't think so."

"Are you talking to me or the bird?"

"You."

"How dare you speak to me that way? I'm not here for myself, you know, Gourd. I've given up a lot to stay and counsel you."

"I know, mother. Thank you."

"You won't visit them, will you?"

"I haven't decided yet."

But the truth is, I have.

I reach out to pet the crow, and he bites at my finger.

"Sorry," I say to the bird.

"I'll forgive you this time," my mother says.

Maybe one day I'll honor my mother and carve her festering blotch of a face into a spirewood log, but for now I feel like tea.

Stepping through the archway into the Thundershine longhouse is almost like stepping into one of my mother's books. The men wear suits. The women wear dresses. The problem is that no one's greeting me with a handshake or even a smile.

I follow the bird, and my bare feet smack against the intricate flowers and vines painted on the stone floor. I try to lighten my step without looking even more stupid. It doesn't work.

As soon as I enter the dining room, the conversations that died when I first entered the house suddenly come back to life behind me.

"Close the door," someone wheezes.

I do as I'm told.

"You're going to regret this," my mother says.

The crow hops onto the table, and the work of art, or what I assumed was a work of art, starts to move. On closer inspection, this skeletal sculpture is actually an old woman, not much more than skin and bones that cling together so tight there's hardly a wrinkle anywhere. Her hand quakes all the way to the bird.

Then the crow speaks, in a soft feminine voice. It says, "Forgive me for not serving you, Gourd. I'm afraid I can't stand." The old woman's lip lines move a little as the bird releases the words.

I pour some tea into a cup painted with elaborate blue flowers that match the old woman's dress. I drink. Rich, warm.

Still my mother says, "She's trying to poison you."

The woman lifts a cup with her free hand, but the shaking causes most of the contents to spill out. A drop or two spatters on the bird. I expect him to fly away or at least flinch. He doesn't.

I'm angry that no one but the bird is here to help this old woman.

"Can I hold your cup for you as you drink?" I say.

"It's alright," she says. "The tea wouldn't do any good for me anyway."

I set my cup down.

"What are they saying to you?" my mother says. "Don't listen to their lies."

"My name is Stone, though most everyone calls me Grandma," she says. "I'm sure your mother spoke of me often."

Hearing the word Grandma is enough to gnarl my innards.

As a child, I hated Grandma Thundershine with a blind intensity that only a child can perfect.

I hated her cruelty. I hated the toys and the cousins she kept away from me. Mostly, I hated my mother's eyes every time she talked about this old woman.

And of course, part of me still does.

"I've invited you here because I'd like to give you a chance to prove yourself," she says. "To prove that you belong with us."

I smile.

I smile at the enemy, because I want smiles and handshakes in return. I want to wear a suit.

"You're talking to her, aren't you?" my mother says. "She'll ruin your life, Gourd. She'll destroy you."

Every wonderful part of life that was taken from my mother exists here, in this house.

"I'm sorry that you and your mother were punished for ideals that have been passed down generation to generation," Grandma says. "It's no one's fault, really. Many hoped that we could finally rid these values from our family once and for all, by keeping you and your mother outside these walls. So that they would die with you." Her hand slides off the crow and rests on the table for a while.

I sit in silence, waiting.

After a few moments, she manages to lift her arm again.

"I understand as much as anyone the benefits of sacrifice," she says. "But I'd rather give you a choice. Luckily, my family feels so guilty about the sacrifices I myself make that they've agreed to honor my request." She closes her eyes. "You should know that this is a dangerous situation, and I do have an alternative motive in asking you to be a part of it." She opens her eyes again. "I'm not very attached to you, Gourd. If you died, I probably wouldn't mourn much at all."

"Better me than a loved one," I say.

She nods. "It's not that I couldn't come to love you. I simply don't know you."

"I understand. I'll do whatever you want." I take a gulp of tea. Strong, cold, like I feel.

But my mother still says, "You can't do this." She sounds like she might start crying, but of course she won't.

She can't.

I expect a claustrophobic desk surrounded by colossal walls of portly books. I expect a clean cut man in glasses wearing a black suit, standing in front of a busy chalkboard. In other words, I expect the illustration on the cover of one of my favorite books growing up: *The Fast Learner*.

I don't expect an underground burrow with a mound of dirt in the center. I don't expect a very short man without a shirt on, sitting on that mound, encircled by candles.

And I don't expect a hug.

"Sit with me," he says.

So I join him inside the circle.

"You're Antash?" I say.

"I'm one who goes by that name, yes. Hopefully you're Gourd and not an Enforcer. Because if I just hugged an Enforcer, I'd need to bathe for a few days, and I don't have time for that."

"I'm Gourd."

"You're a disgrace," my mother says.

Antash grins.

Then the crow hops in from the darkness of the stairway and flies onto a perch that I didn't see before sticking out of the wall.

"It seems Avalanche likes you," Antash says. "He goes where he pleases, and he's come to help you."

"Oh," I say, and try to suppress my smile. He's only a bird after all.

"Before we do anything else, you need to meet Miravel," Antash says.

"Miravel?" I say.

"The Spirit of Life and Death. You haven't heard of him?"

"No."

"Never mind that." He holds my hands. "If he ends up not wanting to work with you, Gourd, don't blame yourself. He's a strange spirit. I've known him for years, and I still don't see any rhyme or reason behind his decisions. The only advice I can really give you is to compliment him on his hair. Other than that, just talk to him."

"I don't know what to say."

"They want you dead," my mother says.

"You'll be fine." Antash closes his eyes and buries his hands in the dirt.

When he opens his eyes again, all the candles burn out, and his pupils illuminate the room with crimson light.

I want my hut.

"You woke me from a very pleasant dream where I was beaching a whale," Antash says. Miravel says.

"I'm sorry," I say.

"Are you going to introduce yourself, or should I call you Dream Spoiler from now on?"

"I'm Gourd."

"Dream Spoiler is more interesting. What am I doing here, Dream Spoiler?"

"I'd like to work with you. Please."

"I could grant your request." His hand thrusts from the earth and clamps my neck. "Or I could kill you."

"Please," I try to say. I also try to pry off his small fingers, but fail at that as well.

"I told you," my mother says.

Avalanche swoops down. He bites and claws at Antash's neck. Miravel's neck.

Miravel releases his grip on my neck, and replaces it with one on the bird's.

Avalanche squirms, squawks, chaws.

I watch.

"You'd let me strangle this bird after he saved you?" Miravel says.

"I don't think I can stop you," I say.

"You're a fool," he says. "I'm in a mortal body with mortal weaknesses."

Still, I watch. I say, "You have nice hair."

I hear a crack. Avalanche collapses, like every villager collapses after an Enforcer finishes the job. And Miravel smiles, the way my mother would smile when she had lips. When she forced me to watch the bloody scene outside the hut.

"Do you still want to work with me?" Miravel says.

"Yes," I say.

I want a suit. I want to stay in this longhouse and never see another villager fall. They make me sick.

Miravel tosses the bird. In mid air, his wings burst with life and he soars to the perch.

"I'll kill you another day, Dream Spoiler," Miravel says, and unearths his hand. The light of his eyes fade.

We sit in the darkness.

I hear weeping.

"Antash?" I say. "Are you hurt?"

"Miravel sends me to my family when he inhabits my body," Antash says. "I can't take the memories back here with me. Only the feelings." He lights a candle, and I can see his tears.

"You're not a Thundershine?" I say.

"No," he says. "But never mind that. We need cockroaches."

Here she is, the key to my salvation: a middle-aged woman named Fireball the Immortal, who even I've heard of. She tosses her wooden sword on my table. Then she sits on my chair by my fire.

"So you're him, huh?" she says.

"I'm him," I say.

"Can you believe the rain out there?" She pulls back her hood, revealing her infamous red hair. It's not as striking as I thought it would be. "This is why I hate coming home." She pulls off her boots. "Do you have any food in here?"

"No."

"Can you get me some? I'm starving."

"Okay." I head for the door.

"On second thought, I'm too tired to eat. Which pile of fur is my bed?"

I point.

"Can you move it closer to the fire?"

I do.

After she's cocooned herself in layers of fur blankets, she says, "How many Enforcers would you say live in those barracks?"

"Maybe twenty," I say, though I know for a fact that there are twenty two. I also know all their names, and they know mine.

"That's too much," she says. "This is going to be horrible. I hope I never wake up."

I worry about how to respond, until I hear her snoring.

"You can't fight the State," my mother says. "You're going to fail. You have to end this now. Use the knife I gave you."

"Goodnight Mother."

Once again, the tiny legs twitch and quiver until they don't twitch and quiver anymore, and Avalanche stares at the cockroach from across the room.

"Are you concentrating?" Antash says.

"Yes," I say.

"Please stop. Consciously, all you need is intent. The rest comes from where your feelings live."

"I can't do this."

"You can." Antash places his hands on my shoulders, gentle, as if I deserve to be touched.

"You told me I'd be ready by now," I say. "And I can't even help a stupid bug."

"They're not stupid, and you will be ready soon. You're simply blocked up inside."

My mother says, "Stick with them, and you're doomed to play with insects the rest of your life. They'll never let you read in the study or dance in the ballroom. They won't share their cologne. They're going to betray you."

Antash holds out his open palm, so I drop the insect on top, because any longer and it would be too late.

In an instant, the cockroach jolts and scuttles off his hand onto the mound of dirt.

In another instant, Avalanche swoops down and swallows the little life whole.

They've done something stupid again, like attempt to hide a shrine in their hut, or speak the name of a demon in front of a snooping Enforcer. I know this because I hear them crying, a man and a woman.

They never learn.

They make me sick.

Fireball ties open the front door flap and sits on my chair, staring outside. She clenches her wooden sword. And her teeth.

She says, "Bastards."

I don't have to watch. My mother isn't forcing me to this time.

Still, I watch as Enforcer Yor smashes a young woman across the head. She falls next to her husband or brother or whoever he is. Heavenly Law states that the beating must end as soon as the culprit loses consciousness. So obviously, the Enforcers avoid the head for as long as possible. It's usually Enforcer Yor who carries out the final blow. He once described himself to my mother as, "The Hand of Mercy."

A little boy with flower petals stuck to his hair clings to his mother's leg. He's been there the whole punishment, and so that leg remains unbloodied and untouched by clubs. The boy, however, drips with his mother's blood, and some of his own. The Enforcers tried to avoid hitting the boy, but no one's perfect.

Enforcer Yor pries the boy loose. He hands him over to an elderly villager and smiles, motioning to the sky. He's saying something about Heaven's plan, I'm sure. And I'm sure no one's listening but himself.

The Enforcers drag the man and woman away, towards the barracks. The boy would follow the trails of blood they leave behind, if he wasn't held down by three other villagers.

Fireball releases her sword. She cries.

I don't.

Yes, the situation outside is a little sad, but it's also normal. It's life.

It's The Way Things Are.

"I'm finishing this tomorrow night," she says. "You better be ready."

"I need more time," I say.

She wipes her face with her sleeve. "Don't talk like that. You're making me nervous."

"I really need more time."

"No, time isn't the secret to accomplishing great things. You just need to take a deep breath, and do what you need to do."

"It's not as simple as that."

"Yes it is. Go do it. But bring me some water first. My mouth is dry."

Antash holds me in his arms, and I wonder if he's like this with all of his students, or if he somehow knows that I'm starving for contact.

It doesn't really matter.

Here, amidst his warmth, I feel different. I cry.

Not for Fireball or Grandma Thundershine or Antash. I cry for myself.

My mother doesn't need to say it. I know I'm going to fail.

Antash clutches my arms and looks me in the eyes. "You must feel very alone, Gourd. I haven't lived your life, but I understand that kind of pain." He takes my hands. "I'm a demon."

That can't be true.

My tears stop.

"Do you know the story of Sin Earth?" Antash says.

"Bits and pieces," I say.

"Well. A long time ago, a demon clan lived on this land. My ancestors. They were very skilled in the demonic arts, but during the Cleansing, most were slaughtered by the Crusaders of Light." He pauses, maybe waiting for me to respond.

I don't.

"The villagers who eventually settled here believed, and still believe, that the blood of my ancestors spilt on this land blessed it with demonic power. A power, they say, that allows them to live the way they want to live. Therefore, the villagers won't stop honoring my kin, no matter what the Enforcers do to them."

The villagers and their resolve make me sick, but I don't say so.

Instead I say, "If your people were slaughtered, how are you here?"

"A few survived," Antash says. "They traveled to a place we call the Hidden Valley and flourished for a while. Then, years ago, we were discovered by the State, and imprisoned for worshipping demons."

"But you are demons."

"According to the Heavenly Texts, demons don't exist. Not anymore. Me and my sister escaped, and she died before the Thundershines found me."

"I'm sorry."

"Thank you." He hugs me again. "You may not feel ready for tonight, but you are. Trust me."

Part of me almost does trust him, but most of me doesn't.

Most of me feels uncomfortable that Antash is a demon. My mother told me the only good that came from demons is the power they discovered.

She said they were simple primitives, like the villagers of Sin Earth, no better than animals. She said they were better off dead.

Most of me leaves the hollow and heads back to my hut. And part of me stays behind, in Antash's arms, amidst his warmth. Feeling different.

Fireball's tears gush forth as she says, "I don't want to do this. I hate this. I hate this!" She throws her wooden sword across the room and knocks over one of my mother's books: *Dancing Etiquette for Wedding Ceremonies.*

I walk over to replace the book, but decide to leave it in the dirt instead.

Fireball curls up on her bed. She sobs even louder.

I walk over to kneel by her, to place a hand on her shoulder. But I cross my arms and stand there instead. I'm not Antash.

Avalanche steps off my mother's chair and soars down beside Fireball. He pecks at her arm.

"Stop that, Avalanche," she says.

He doesn't.

"Stop it!" She stands and straightens her tunic. "You know, for a god, you're really annoying."

Avalanche squawks.

"What do you mean god?" I say.

"He's a god," she says. "He's Miravel's children. Miravel had four children, but they all sort of joined together into one being. It's complicated."

"Why are they stuck in that body?"

"They're not." She picks up her sword. "I'm ready to go now." She ties her hair back with a string, then steps outside.

I follow.

The villagers dance around two bonfires tonight, and somehow I know they're honoring trees. Fireball walks out into the clearing between the two fires and waits.

The singing stops. The dancing stops. All eyes focus on Fireball.

I remain at the outside of the clearing, with Avalanche on a nearby blueburst branch.

Fireball points her sword at a couple of Enforcers standing outside the barracks. "Tell your commander I'm here," she says.

They look at each other and go inside.

Fireball's nothing like the bawling mess I witnessed only moments ago. She's like a statue now. Solid, stable.

Still my mother says, "They're going to destroy her."

Enforcer Yor, and every other Enforcer in the village, exit the barracks and form a line between Fireball and the building.

"Welcome to our little village, stranger," Enforcer Yor says, and approaches Fireball. "If there's anything the State can do to make your stay more comfortable, please let us know."

"Leave here and never return," Fireball says. In the light of these bonfires, her hair is more than striking.

Enforcer Yor grins. "How could we rid the world of demonic remnants if we left, my dear?"

"You couldn't. You have no right to be here."

"We have every right that matters."

"I won't let you have Sin Earth."

"There's nothing you can do, sweetheart. It will be ours."

Heavenly Law states that land isn't hereditary. Not anymore.

Property reverts to the State when the owner dies.

When Grandma Thundershine dies.

Fireball points her sword at Enforcer Yor's face. The Enforcers immediately drop their clubs and draw their sacred blades.

"If you touch us in violence we have the right to use lethal force," Enforcer Yor says.

"It won't matter what you do to me," she says. "I'm Fireball the Immortal."

"No you're not." Enforcer Yor keeps his smile on, but his eyes look frightened.

According to the Heavenly Texts, there's no such person as Fireball the Immortal. She's a myth created by simple-minded villagers.

Fireball lifts her necklace from under her shirt and reveals a whistle. She blows.

A flurry of white fur rushes from the forest. I stand, shaking, as the enormous monkeys race past me to the middle of the clearing.

"The demon gods have come to fight for their people," Fireball says.

"There are no demons," Enforcer Yor says. "The Heavens cleansed them from the earth long ago."

"Will you leave this place?"

Enforcer Yor's smile fades. "No."

There's a short pause, and then the battle begins.

The Enforcers use their metal. Fireball and the monkeys use their wood.

The villagers watch because to fight would change them from the People of Sin Earth into something else.

And me, I close my eyes.

I hear screams and shouts and thuds and groans. I hear Avalanche's squawking. I hear crying. I hear my mother's bitter silence.

"Gourd!" Fireball says. "Help her! Hurry!"

I open my eyes and scream as a giant monkey charges right at me. He hurries past me, dragging a monkey behind him. He leaves the body behind a tree.

"Help her!" Fireball says.

I walk behind the tree and stare at the monkey. She's bleeding from the neck.

I kneel. I place my hand on her bloodied fur.

I wait.

After a while, it's too late. I step out from behind the tree.

"Where is she?" Fireball says.

I stare at her. Her worst cut is on her nose. What's left of her nose anyway.

"Gourd!" Fireball says.

"I couldn't do it," I say. "I'm sorry."

Fireball growls and rejoins the battle.

I watch as Enforcer Yor runs up behind Fireball. I could shout out for her to look out, but I don't. This is the way it has to be.

After Fireball falls, a monkey carries her into my hut, and I follow. I'm afraid one of those things would smash my head in if I didn't.

The monkey grunts at me, then leaves.

I kneel beside Fireball.

I place my hand on her.

I wait.

I can't do this.

"Gourd," a voice says behind me.

I turn around and smile.

He's here.

He's here to save me.

He smiles at me and drinks from a tiny cup. Then he falls to the ground.

"Antash!" I say.

I check his body. He's dead.

I place my hands on his chest. His warmth is disappearing.

I'm a bawling mess. Shaky, broken.

Still my mother says, "You make me sick."

I stand and face my mother's chair, though I can't see her there. "You make me sick, Mother," I say, breaking through my sobs.

"How dare you—"

"You could have left this village to start a new life. We could have been happy, but you stayed here to take your anger out on these people." I reach under the table and retrieve the sacred club. "You spied on them. You lied about them. You got them beaten and imprisoned. You separated parents from their children. You make me sick!" I smash her chair, over and over. Then I throw the sacred club out the door.

"If you don't apologize, I'm going to disown—"

"Shut up, mother!"

And finally, she's gone.

I place my hands on Antash's chest again and remember the first time my mother forced me to sit on her chair, and watch through the doorway as a villager was attacked. The villager's name was Kyar.

Back then, I didn't hold back my tears.

Back then, I wasn't afraid to care.

My mother slapped me. "Don't you dare cry for them, Gourd," she said. "They're the reason we're stuck out here."

But I didn't feel stuck.

I liked when Kyar taught me how to dance, and Vyen taught me how to sing. I liked playing with Bayarg and Chirwa. I was only a little boy, but I liked my home. I liked my people.

My mother thought the Thundershines were wasting their powers on these simple primitives, no better than animals.

I don't.

Thundershines, demons, spirits, villagers, animals. I'll fight for the good of them all.

Anytime someone uses Miravel's power, there's a chance the spirit god will take the life of the caster.

Still, I take the chance.

Miravel's power rushes through the ground into my feet, through my body, out my fingertips.

Antash opens his eyes.

I spin around and place my hands on Fireball.

I'm afraid it's too late, but I allow Miravel's power to flow through me anyway.

I wait for death.

It doesn't come, however, and Fireball opens her eyes and breathes.

"I hate dying," she says. Then she hugs me. "Let's finish this"

Me and Antash follow her outside.

She blows her whistle, and the gigantic monkeys retreat to the forest.

The still conscious Enforcers stare at Fireball the Immortal. She's alive and unwounded.

She points her sword. "Leave here and never return."

"I think we've done all we can here," Enforcer Yor says. "We should return to the Capital."

"Release your captives, then go."

The Enforcers walk and limp into the barracks.

After a short time, dirty and emaciated villagers leave the building. Even in their weak state, they hurry toward the others.

Family's reunite.

Enforcers retreat.

Avalanche lands nearby, dotted with blood, and I feed him some spicenuts I kept in my pocket.

As I smile, a memory bursts in my mind. I remember a spirit I played with as a young child. My mother told me he was imaginary. She told me to forget about him, and eventually I did. He was a crow.

I look around for Fireball, but don't see her. I have a feeling she's behind a tree, crying over the body of an old friend.

"We should say goodbye to Grandma Thundershine before I release her," Antash says.

"Release her?" I say.

"Her time to enter the spirit world was a long time ago, but she asked me to keep her alive. Her life was the only thing keeping the State from devastating this land. The villagers would have been driven out. The forest would have been annihilated. The earth itself would have died. But now we're safe again."

I'm afraid that the Enforcers will return, but I know Antash is right.

The Heavenly Texts state that there's no such person as Fireball the Immortal. There are no demons anymore. No demonic powers. There are only simple worshippers with primitive minds, who need to be converted and civilized.

And so, when something contradicts the Heavenly Texts, the State destroys it. And when it can't be destroyed, the State does its best to ignore it.

The Enforcers won't come back.

"Antash," I say.

My mother says nothing.

I'm not afraid to care anymore.

I take a deep breath, and do what I need to do.

Antash smiles.

THE RULES

First, test the accused with a kitten or a bunny—preferably one that you've taken care of for a few days. Don't hesitate to name it after one of your own children, if you have any.

"We're not them," the man says, again.

Although at this point, of course, you're convinced he isn't a man. He's sweating and trembling, the way all demons do.

Still, part of you hopes your instincts are wrong. Sara's an innocent in all this, and you like how she purrs in your arms, trusting you the way you'd never trust anyone.

Nevertheless, Sara is a lesser being. Her purpose on this planet to is to be used, and nothing more.

So you continue to wait, knowing that demons can't control their most basic impulses.

Like a stab in the gut, you feel the foreign presence penetrate your body. You feel the dark essence worm its way up your chest, into your arms, your hands, and then it happens.

You grit your teeth, twisting Sara's head until it snaps. Hot urine sprays on your tunic.

You toss Sara aside.

Before the demons can make another move, you put on your amulet and say, "Try that again."

"I didn't do it," the demon says.

You spit out a laugh.

"Please," he says. "Let my children go."

You glance at the spawn in the corner, and you seem to have tied one of them too tight, because she's purple and writhing on the floor.

As soon as the father notices this, he screams. He howls with tears.

Now's the time to remember the most important rules, because these demons will hit you with spells that fill you with guilt and shame and disgust. They'll make you feel like the vermin they are. They might even convince you that you killed Sara yourself.

Ignore any tears, even your own.

When you're carving them with the sacred blades, they'll beg for mercy, the way all demons do.

Wear earplugs if you have to.

The spawn pleads in silence, squeezing her dead sister.

Expect a lot of blood.

And never, ever look them in the eyes.

Trust me.

FLAPJACK

WALL #4'S BUMPY blemish showed me an environment capable of imperfection, and yet the Prisoners, AKA the Wee-the-People, AKA the Captivated Captivitized saw eternal only the wrongness of their own little selves. Of course, my thinker could produce not a one example to justify such sham-shame thoughts. These Wee ones never harmed each other. They had chances many, oh hai, but caused not a bloody scratch with their forenails. They were Hopper Lites (meaning wimps), the lot of them, just like me.

Once my cellmate Humpty ran his mind so far downwards, listing that and that and that his Sin, that I couldn't take it anymore, and I said, "I'm so sick and tired of your blubbering blubbery cheeks!"

He cried with crinklier eyelids. "I must be the worst man in the world to be yelled at by one of us."

"The Flapjack is filled with much worse!" You must keep in mind that rarely ever had I erupted such fury—the truth being I'd never known such a pitiful creature as this Humpty in my life.

His whimpering shrunk to a sniffle in a bug-flap. He stared at me, not with anger (as I expected, since I had just spoken blasphemy), but with fear. If Wall #2 wasn't blocking him, he might have kept walking backward until I twinkled out of sight.

My body trembled as my anger trickled down. More than anything, I wanted to alleviate his anguish, so I resolved to tell him the tippy truth. "It's not what you think, Humpty. I speak from experience. I'm from the Flapjack."

He laughed awkward through his nose, and mumbled something like, "Verily not."

"I know you don't believe me and that's fine for now. But I'm begging you to stop pleading so much."

"A prayer in the mind is worth nada," which was something I was beginning to understand about the Wee-the-People. They preferred speaking out loud—to walls, to floors, to anything inanimate. Speaking to other people was just as worthless as thinking to one's own self.

"Could you try to be quieter then?" said I.

Humpty stood from his knees. A sort of smirk tugged at his lips. "You've been so silent ever since you came here…I assumed you were a mighty careful man. I thought verily that you kept your body and mind tippy pure. But perhaps your lack of prayer has more to do with lack of care. Verily. I shall have to pray for you as well as I, as would any good-bearing man."

"I appreciate your concern, but praying isn't going to help either of us. If you verily care about my concordia, then allow me your ears for a short tiempo. I need to speak to a person."

"You're a strange man, Newton, but hai. I'll harken, for harmony's sake." His face then metamorphosized before my peepers, with a new exhibition of expression he had never shown before. Some might dub it interest or even curiosity. I, however, would call it waking up.

My first rememberable memory, I told Humpty, involved a thing which I at first mistook for an unwrapped candy-dandy, but was verily my sister's severed thumb. My father held the stained feeler close to my nose and said, "See this? Do you smell it, child?" Then he lifted me higher and higher and higher to his tippy reach, onto his shoulder, so I could say hello to the bloody beddy bye, where my sister wriggled. The tear on her face melted me, but my tearburst was silenced by my father's stone hand, and, "Hush child! This is your sister's time."

So I watched in silence, fighting myself, as my mother applied skin glue to my sister's wound. "Do you see what the Greens have done to her?" my father said. "Do you see?!?"

I opened my mouth and might have said, "Hai."

Gloria, my sister, only then seemed to notice me. She smiled a little, sickly sweet, as if to say, "I'm glad you're with me now, but I'm so sorry you're with me now." I was whooshed back down to the floor, and covered my sniffer, afraid my father would stick baby pinky back in front of me. But he didn't. Instead, my familia—my mother, my father, Granner, Gramper, Uncer, Aunter, and others—hugged Gloria. They said things like, "You're a real woman now," and, "The first one is the hardest."

Solus, I felt—being the #1 and only child in the room. The second youngest person was Gloria, who was at the time about fourteen. Far ahead than poor smally me. Soon, everyone said their goodbyes and left, except Gloria and my mother. I, of course, remained stuck to the ground, as if the bottoms of my feet had been ripped off and skin glue was applied before I landed.

"Take your sibber with you when you go," my mother said to my sister. "Do you feel dizzy when you stand?"

Gloria stood and shook her head.

"Good," said my mother. "Go when you're ready."

"I'm ready," my sister said.

So Gloria clutched my hand with her fivey, and led me into the hallway.

Just moments ago, I'd felt like I was in a monsterworld, where my familia wasn't really my familia. I'd felt like I wanted to leave. But now that I was actually leaving, I felt a thunder urge to run to my parents' beddy bye and hide under the coverings. My mother's words, "Take your sibber with you when you go," I took to mean that me and my sister were leaving eternal. So I released my tearburst and yanked to free myself.

She only held on mightier. "Sibber, stop. We're only going outside for a minuto, then we'll come right back."

I stopped struggling, though I didn't believe her verily. But the tranquility of her voice calmed me.

She pushed the sliding door with her foursies, very careful. We went into the backyard, and she led me to the sad drooping tree. We sat together.

She started to dig a hole with her fivey. "You can help me if you want."

So I did. Every scoop intensified the cold nothingness in my feelers. "That's enough," she said. And she held out her foursies. Only then did I notice that she was clutching her separated part. She dropped it into the hole. And while we covered it with dirt, we had a conversation something like this:

"It doesn't hurt too much, sibber," she said. "You don't have to feel sorry for me. Things like this happen all the time."

"How come there was blood?" said I. "The Body Fairy makes the parts go whoosh with no blood."

"Sibber. There's...no such thing as the Body Fairy."

When I breathed out, I saw a little fairy form in my cold air. "Then where do all the parts go?" Of course, I should have known the answer to that, considering what we were doing at that very momento.

"The Green familia does it, sibber. They cut us. That's what happened to all of Mommy and Granner and Aunter and everyone's parts. There's no Body Fairy."

"But...why do the Greens do that?"

"Because we're at war with them. They cut us and we cut them."

"Why?"

"You don't have to worry about that now. Nobody's going to chop your parts until you're my age. So don't worry."

And the truth is, though it seems ridiculous, the momento I returned to the house, to my room, to my beddy bye, I did stop worrying. I went back to having a tippy unstressed childhood, except for the one little idea aft of my mind that Thumbelina the Body Fairy was dead and buried in the backyard under the crying tree. Crying, because I knew that one day my life would change.

I trotted downstairs in the white tunic, thinking blue, pink, blue, pink, and then pondering how little I cared. The living room ravaged my nose with hospital-smell, but the stinkeroo turned out to be emanating from the plastic wrapping around the furniture and tele and even the floor. My ceremonial place was in the center of the room, so there I stood. After they sang the Happy, Happy Self Day song (verily badly), my father said, "You are a boy." I closed my eyes and pinched my nose as they splashed me with smally paint balloons. My white tunic stained blue. However, this was not the same blue tunic I would wear for special occasions the rest of my life, as I'd first assumed. My father would soon give me a different wearable blue tunic, while my painted blue tunic would remain unworn eternal.

After I showered and the plastic wrappers were thrown away, we ate cake. I knelt beside my sister, and watched her grip the fork with the only three fingers on her right hand. Soon, she'd have to be fed by a man, like the other older women. By that time, she'd be married.

"Do you feel any different?" my mother said.

"Not verily," said I.

"You can start growing out your hair now. Aren't you hypered?"

I wasn't really excited, but I nodded my baldness anyway.

My father stopped feeding my mother, and stood. "It's about tiempo this smally boy has a name, sure enough?" He walked behind me and placed a hand on my shoulder. "We have decided his name to be Newton."

"Hello Newton!" everyone said, but me.

My father continued, "As we all know, every given name has a double meaning. First, Newton is the name for someone intelligent, and we all must agree that my smally boy here is intelligent." (The familia agreed with yeses and nods.) "The second meaning is that he has a prox relationship with gravity."

Everyone laughed, and I smiled.

What they were saying, of course, was that I had a great frequency for falling—tripping, even when there was nothing on the ground to trip me. Ergo, I thought my name captured both my tippy and bottom traits. Though I soon came to understand that my lack of coordination didn't worry my familia one whittle whit. My father once told me, "Boys like you will probably never become a samurai, or gladiator, or wrestler, or knight,

but you can still become a mighty crazy horse. Even wild randomness had
its place in war, son."

Anyway, though the slight majority of children born with inward
genitalia were made women, I was made a boy named Newton.

You can imagine my surprise when Humpty interrupted me with, "And...
and where was I during all this?"

"Where were *you?*" said I.

"Hai. What was I doing, I mean. Did I eat the cake? Did I throw those
balloons at you? And if so, what did they feel like in my hands? What did
the cake taste like?"

He continued on like this, in ramble. One might—if one hadn't seen
the laetitia, the tippy happiness, in his peepers— have mistaken his words
as spawns of sarcasm or teasing.

Obvious to me then, he didn't believe a word I was saying. But he liked
the words. Verily. Enough to want to be a part of them.

"Hai, Humpty, you were there," said I. "Invisible though, you were
at the time. Invisible to everyone but I. You were my best amicus for life.
Eternal."

"And what do I...did I look like, if I may ask?"

"Oh tippy beautiful, Humpty. The most beautiful woman on the whole
Flapjack. But when they looked at you, they couldn't see that."

"I thought you said I was invisible."

"You were, at the time of the party. Things would change in time."

"But things never change."

"Hai, verily they do not. But sometimes they can."

My mother looked down at my bloody beddy bye coverings. "It's nothing to be
afraid of, Newton. That's the blood of our ancestors. Let's go tell your father."

We went into the family room and my mother forced me in front of
the tele.

"Haste, Newton, what is it?" my father said.

"There's blood on my bed," said I. For some reason, fear clutched my tum. I half expected him to yell at me or even slap me.

Instead, he happy-faced. "Newton, that's great!" He turned off the tele. After a biggy bear-hug, he said, "That blood came out to say that tonight you'll become a man."

I forced a smile, but I remembered Gloria's Thumbelina—though it was only women who lost parts. What then, would I lose?

That night instructed, dressed in the blue tunic my father had given me, I met the other men in the front yard. Before a word could pop my lips, they led me down the street to the house I'd passed mucho tiempos to and fro the gymnasium: the Green House. Mightily, I'd heard from my familia how ug this place was. Into the courtyard we went, and true enough, the stories reflected proper this wild place that zapped my peepers and nostrils. Bitter-stinking weeds where the grass should've been, some taller than I, swayed with the airbursts. Nearby, the forgotten forget-me-nots shivered. In the center court, a lady with red spots all over her clothes and skin froze in mid-step. Water was supposed to spurt from her mouth, but didn't. And even though she lacked feelers and toes and even ears, if I squinted my peepers, the vines that grew up around her formed new feelers and toes and even ears. My familia hated this place, but I wanted to sit by the lady and harken her silent stories.

Instead, my father led me toward one of the personal quarters that lined the courtyard. My Uncer and Gramper and some Cousers whooshed past, and entered first. By the time my father and I went inside, my familia had secured a young woman to her beddy bye. They gripped her wriggling arms and legs. They covered her mouth with tight cloth.

My father and I stood beside her. He held out a cutter. After my hesitation, he said, "Take it."

So I did. And as I did, the flank of familiarity caused a buzz in my mind. So known was this momento because I'd been preparing for it all my life. The games the young baldies played in the gymnasium ricocheted through my skull. Cutty me, I cutty you—cut, cut, to, fro, on, on, anon.

"Take a feeler, Newton," said my father. "The same feeler they took from Gloria. Think about the pain she felt that night. Think about her tears. Think about the blood. Punish them, Newton, for what they've done. Punish them!" The words rumbled through his teeth, and I saw spit backflip off his lip onto the young woman's arm.

My vision crept from the spittle spot up to her peepers. She was mightily verily terrored. Hai, I did think about Gloria's pain, but the Red—the fury of my ancestors—didn't ignite in my own peepers. Instead, the spotted fountain lady awoke in my mind, and someone slashed at her viney feelers and toes and ears. With a cough, cough, cough, blood gushed from her wide-o mouth.

I dropped the cutter, whoosh, and the Red-spotted lady (as well as the young girl on the beddy bye) happy-faced.

Morning, and my courtyard sparkled clean, clean, clean with shimmer stones and flatty grass. Our fountain maiden gurgled in missing-bits ecstasy of spread arms. But nada of that mattered a whittle whit, because I stood outside the quarters of my parents and harkened.

"He's just not ready yet," said my mother.

"Verily so," said my father.

"These things happen, Maximus."

"Hai, but not in my familia."

"Don't give me that holier-than. Some tiempo is all Newton needs. A few weeks and he'll be ready."

"If he fails again..."

"He won't."

The words bit at me too ravagely, so I backed away. Without forethinking, I rat-a-tatted on my sister's door. Her hubber Francis helloed and let me inside.

"Salu, Newton," Gloria said, on the center-mat.

I knelt beside her. "Did you hear?"

"Hai."

Francis served her tea, completely—the way a man did for his fingerless wife.

"Why didn't you do it?" she said.

"I...couldn't," said I. "I don't know what happened."

Francis brought the cup close to her mouth, but she shook her head and he scooted away a little.

"You should've just done it and got it over with, sibber," she said. "It's not hard what you have to do. Have you thought about what I've gone through? Have you? Do you know what they've done to me!?!" Her face shook. "Cham the Greens!"

"Gomen, Gloria," said I, my blurred vision drowning in my tea cup.

"Sorries don't change anything," she said, and calmed her breathing, iiiiin ouuuuut. "I'm not mad at you. Verily, I'm not. But you're part of this familia. Whatever it is that stopped you last night, let it flitter, flitter away. Concentrate on the Red."

I tried—verily, I did, to find the Red, find the Red, find the Red. But when I closed my peepers, all I saw was Green, held down, trembling, and the young girl's pupils that vibrated in a way like bugs trapped behind glass.

Prox to sleep in my beddy bye that night, I saw my amicus eternal, clearer than I'd seen her for years and years and years. And let's say, for the sake of sakes, that her name was Humpty. Let's also say that she looked a little like the fountain maiden at the Green house, except her feelers and toes and ears were not made of blurry squinty vines, but feelers and toes and ears.

"Cheeks up, Newt," Humpty said, happy-faced beside my beddy bye. "So you didn't chop her. So what? It's not the end of Flapjack."

"My father hates me," said I.

"Mayhaps, mayhaps not. But what matters is that I got what I wanted, true enough?"

"What do you mean?"

"Verily you're joking."

"Iie, I'm not."

She piggle-giggled (with a snort), and said, "I made you whoosh down that cutter, of course. I whispered those dreadful thoughts right into your listen-hole."

"Why?"

"What do you mean why? You know as well as I do, I hate all that bloody blood chop chop stuff. Cham it all to heckles."

"You didn't used to say words like cham."

"Hai, but I'm a growing young woman, true enough? You should see the size of my twiddly-wink."

"Sick, Humpty. Don't talk like that."

"Gomen, gomen." She bowed. "Anywho, I'd better be off and hit that dusty hobo, as they say."

"No one says that."

"You're obviously not yapping the right people. Well, sayonara, Newty-chan."

"Wait, where are you going?"

Before her mouth could pop another word, she whooshed into the floor. Verily, I hadn't spoken to Humpty and she hadn't spoken to me for a mighty tiempo. But she'd always known how to lift my cheeks. And even now, both of us grown and sprouting, she helped me forget my lack of Red, even when I felt—

Humpty the Prisoner's tearburst caused me to pause my tale. He collapsed to his knees and said, "Deserve I don't such a thing as this. Verily, verily, verily I do not."

"What is it you're talking about?" said I.

"These things are for the Flapjack, not Wee-the-People. Temptation has poisoned my concordia. I only hope I can purge your words from me. But will they shatter my honored nightmares and haunt me with laetitia dreams eternal?" He quivered on the floor.

"The story has only begun, Humpty."

"Humpty? Humpty?!? Who is that you speak of? I have no spoken name, for you have sucked away its purity."

"Then I shall have to tell my story to the void you have become, true enough?"

"Iie! Even a void knows its place."

"I see. So you'll never hear whether or not I ever became a man. You'll never hear how it was you became a real person who all real people could see. I suppose I'll count to three now, and then never, ever, ever speak again eternal. One mississippi, two mississippi, three—"

"Hold!" He pushed himself up and sat. "Mayhaps...mayhaps I'm meant to hear your story, then struggle to recover. Mayhaps this is a test of my concordia. Mayhaps you can continue on anon."

"Hai," and that I did.

The days following the mishap at the Green house felt like ground up wildflowers. Blooming rainbows burst and burst and burst into my mind, but every tiempo Humpty made me feel concordia and laetitia, my familia would hack away with a chop chop chop, wielding their sharper-than-sharp silences. For instance, when I walked into the dining room to dine, my familia would shush-up with a bug-flap. Oh, what a difference it would've made if they'd pointed their feelers or nubs at me and said, "A bloody Hopper Lite, you are!" or "Coward child, go cham yourself!" But no, my bloody Redless failure of a night was too titmouse even for open rabble-rouse ranting. So they kept their lips as tight lines. Lines that read: You are solus.

One night my Couser Betty helloed in my quarters.

"Salu, Betty."

She clicked the door behind her, and stood by my beddy bye. "Newton...I..."

"Betty, what's wrong?"

"I..."

In my thinker, I imagined she was going to boom a tearburst, but instead she roared like some trollbeast. She sat beside me. Her hands shivered and her face vibrated.

"What's wrong, Betty?"

"I...never had a sibber of my own," she said. "You've been the closest thing to a sibber I've had."

"Hai, you've been like a little sibber to me."

"I don't want to bother you, but there's no one else I can turn to."

"Don't worry about that, Betty. If there's something inside you that needs letting, let it out to me."

"Well...it's Uncer Matty. He used to...bounce me."

"What?" Uncer Matty was a man Uncer to the both of us.

"Hai, he bounced me. Cham him!"

"I'm so sorry, Betty. Have you told your parents?"

"You know as well as I do, it wouldn't matter if I did or not. They can't do anything to him."

"We have to stop him somehow."

"Stop him?!?" She laughed with gritted teeth. "He doesn't come around anymore since I reached the Red. He knows I'd bite his chamming face off." It was true. Betty had become a woman recently. Skin glue shined on her new finger-ghost. "So really, there's nada I can do, unless he enters my quarters. And he won't. He's a Hopper Lite at heart."

The words Hopper Lite thrashed me, and Betty must have noticed.

She clutched my hand. "I don't believe what the familia is saying about you. You may have dropped the cutter, but you're not like Uncer Matty. Even as a boy, you're a better man than him."

"I...I'd like to help you, Betty. But what can I do?" Hai, I asked the question, though I knew the answer.

Even then, my thinker and body were not animated by Red. Hai, I felt sorry for Betty in the tippiest, but, as pathetic as it seemed to me then, all I wanted was to forget Betty's pain. I wanted to grab Betty's hand and fly her into the dreambubbles above my beddy bye where Humpty lived. We'd play and play and play on the wildflowers, but no matter how many stomps we'd plant on the planties, they'd spring back up like a new spring eternal.

The only alternative to taking her to the dreambubble that I knew about was bloody Red cut cut.

"There must be another way, Newtrino," Humpty said, springing, springing, springing on the biggy marshymallow. "Why don't you ask those bloody blockbrained mommer and popper of yours?"

"Betty's right. Uncer Matty and them are the same gener. They can't do anything."

"So now you have to?"

"Hai."

"But you're a Hopper Lite."

"Iie."

"Just accept it and go eat some parsnips."

"Iie!"

The dreambubble popped, and for a while I labored to piece Humpty together again. But it was a puzzle of shattered butterflies and my feelers were too big. In other more thinkable words, no matter how verily Humpty was my amicus eternal, my familia was my familia.

So outside I went with heavy zombie limbs, but soon the nippy airbursts reached in my yapper and yanked the nightsickness right out. I tip-toe tapped into my Uncer Matty's quarters. Closer, closer, closer I slushed, careful as careful can be. But gravity played another one of its tricks, and my face slapped the wooden floor. I heard Uncer Matty rustle.

My face still pressed, I didn't know if he was looking down at me or not, but I didn't move. Somehow, all the bitter silence my familia had force-fed me seemed to radiate deep inside my gut now. I used this internal-quiet to transform into a waterless fountain statue, like the one at the Greens. Only this time, the statue was not beautiful.

After perhaps an hora, I convinced myself that Uncer Matty wasn't staring down at me with burning dragon eyes, and pushed myself up. I stood slow and awkward in a way that felt like a growing tree.

On the table by his beddy bye, a cutter smiled, reflecting white moon-teeth. I touched it and didn't pick it up for a long while. Still, Red didn't urge me on or thank me. No one lifted the cutter but little me.

I peeled away Uncer Matty's beddy bye coverings, then his body's coverings. I wanted Humpty to speak to me then. I wanted her to break out of the fountain maiden outside the door like a chicky from a shell, and then run in and save me. But I heard not a word. All I saw were Uncer Matty's peepers that stayed straight black lines. Lines that read Betty's answer to my question: "Chop that tinkerdam twiddly-wink of his, so I can give it a proper burial."

"Why do you hold?" Humpty said in his smally Wee-the-People voice.

"Because that's the end of that tale," said I. "I'm trying to decide where the next story of my life begins."

"The end, you say? That it was not."

"If I were speaking a prayer, then hai, it would not be the end. So hear this amen and calm yourself: amen."

"That's not enough."

"Praise be my suffering, amen. Is that better?"

"Did you chop him or didn't you?!?"

"If you hadn't noticed, Humpty, the stories I've been telling you have been going in the order of my life. Therefore, the next story I tell you will be an older me than before. I will either be someone-who-chopped-my-uncer-in-the-past, or someone-who- didn't-chop-my-uncer-in-the-past. Don't you think you'd be able to tell the difference between those two people?"

"I..."

"Rhetorical questions are answered by those who ask them, Humpty, so rest your yapper."

He rubbed at his forehead like he was trying to erase something. Finally, he said, "I'm sorry."

"What about?"

"When you were in your Uncer's room, you wanted Humpty to come in and save you. I'm sorry I...I'm sorry that Humpty wasn't there for you. I'm sure she would have helped you if she could."

"Verily so."

In the dining room, Red swirly-whirled in Uncer Matty's peepers as they did everyever he and me were prox. My familia perceived his peepers as two cycloid mirrors that reflected my own Redness, where things looked even less mighty than they verily were. So sat Newton the Red Man, Hero of and to the Familia.

On the left of me knelt Betty, (that being her chosen place now), and on the right knelt Venus, a young woman with outside genitalia—the newest dinner guest of my father, though of course he invited her not for his own self.

"Can you help me with something, Newton-san?" my Uncer Edo said from across the table.

"Hai," said I.

"My thinker wishes to acquire a new cutter, but I'm halted between the Bane and the Lance. Which model do you prefer, nepher-san?"

The differences between those blades I neither awared nor cared, but "The Bane," said I, the false prophet.

"Hai," my Uncer Edo said. "An older model, but proven mighty."

"Newton-san speaks wise," my father said, anod. "Hai, there is a place for new innovations, but when it comes to war, it is trust most important to familia. I trust the Bane as I trust my son."

"Verily so. I shall take Newton-san's advice," my Uncer said.

After a few momentos, Venus fumbled with her teacup, though she was only missing two feelers on that hand. She set the cup down and turned to me. "Newton-san, could you help with my drink? My familia uses a different sort of cup, and my poor touchers can't seem to get a hold of this one."

That wasn't true, of course, but I obliged. I brought the cup close to her lips and she sipped. My familia watched and one of my Uncers—I know not which—made a hissy-whistle to tease me.

Verily, part of why I served Venus her tea was because Venus and my familia expected such, but the other part had to do with my own horndoggy throbby. To serve a woman meant also to serve oneself.

"Thank you," she said. And in my freakshow thinker, those words implied gratitude for the dreambubbles whooshing out my peepers that replaced her missing parts with those I'd chopped from the beautiful Green butterflies quivering under a bloodmoon.

"Iie," Humpty said, his arms and eyeroofs diagonal.

"Pardon?" said I.

"Mayhaps you did chop your Uncer, but chop the young Greens, you did not. Return and change your words."

"That I cannot."

"Words can be changed as stains can be cleansed."

"Hai, speak I mutable words, but the events their own selves remain stone. Mayhaps you don't believe this to be my life's tale, but that it is my tale, you can't deny. Unless you believe my form and manner projected from your mind."

"Impure notion! I am my own self. You yours."

"Then allow me my own words."

Slow, he uncrossed himself and was open like a day-flower once again.

One might expect that acceptance would bring with it a lesser need for Humpty, but iie—the tighter they embraced me, the more I suffocated and yearned for fresh fairy-air. Night eternal, Humpty and I trotted through misadventurous meadows, but that was not enough. I needed tippy tippy tippy more, like a spiral-bearing druggy on neon brain-worms.

Viz, nearly all my semi-wake horas I spent at the comper in my quarters, talkathoning with Humpty through the rat-a-tat pecking of my touchers.

Often we spent our tiempo in the teahouse of my mind. There, mucho men thronged about the smally geisha, who wore patterns of open wounds and heroes of old and shimmering blades.

"These women are mightily ug, true enough?" Humpty said. She sat at the table thighs aslant, like the men about.

"They're considered tippy beautiful by most," said I, and watched one such man hold a hanky close to a geisha's sniffer so she could sniffle out.

"Professional amputations a beauty makes?" Humpty said. It was true. The geisha had their entire arms and legs removed at a very young age to become less and more than any other woman.

"There's mas to their art than missing parts, Humpty. They're trained to speak the words a man wants to harken."

"Shock! Men desire to harken a woman's words? Why then do they hum when I open my yapper?"

"I'm only playing the devil's advocate."

"Advocate or avocation did you say? I cannot hear you mighty what with the chitchat and razzmatazz swarming."

"You'll never get betrothed with that attitude," said I.

"And what would I do with a hubber? Do I not have feelers and feet unbroken to serve my needs and wants?"

"Verily so."

"Then slow yourself to spew me pity, for I stink enough from sleeping in a tree."

"You're jesting, true enough?"

"Iie. I ran away from my familia before our enemies had the chance to chop me, and I've slept in a tree that day eternal, with a moat and traps circum. And if they manage to breach those barriers, everyever I'll have sharpened parsnips to pitch at their chumming faces."

I laughed, then turned my happyface down. "Does such a life not make you feel solus?"

"I have you."

"Verily so."

And I noticed two things then. One: a group of men were standing circum Humpty, pointing feelers, hahaing, speaking words like ug and mannish. And two: Humpty didn't care.

And Humpty the Prisoner said, "If Humpty cared not what spawned in the thinkers of others, then why is it you could not be the same way?"

"There it is," said I. "The question of questions."

"That's all you give me? Another bland statement drowning in abstraction?"

"I see. So you wish to be served answer after answer after answer as a man would serve a geisha, true enough? That sounds very unHumptylike to me."

"Even Humpty my thinker imagines would at tiempos grow weary of your riddles."

"My riddles?!? You name the question born from your own mind: Newton's Problem? Take some responsibility."

"And how does one go about doing that?"

"Start off by naming your own brainchild after yourself. Humpty Junior or Humptina, if you like. Then answer their questions when they ask you."

"What if I know not what to reply?"

"Make it up as real parents do. The important thing isn't that you're right, but that they shut up their yappers. Otherwise, how will you ever sleep?"

"I don't think I'm ready to be a brainparent."

"Well don't look at me. I have my own children to feed."

"I say I'm not ready!" He repositioned to his knees and locked his feelers.

"Pray not! To hear a parent's worries brings only suffering and greater agitation to a child. But worry not, for I have a known remedy. Allow me to continue my tale, and soon your child will fall to sleep. Then you'll have tiempo to your own self once more."

He nodded, and for both our thinker-children, proceeded I in lullaby.

An e-Hermes soared into my comper vision and proclaimed, "Salutations and congratulations! Your Site has just become one of the tippy hundred on all Flapjack." My Site, you see, had been—for quite a mighty tiempo—devoted lock, stock and bottomless barrel to the Humpty-and-me Semigoodtime Adventures in Mundane Land. Not that I verily cared to make our talky intercourses public, but I had nada else to put on my Site, since this specific composing gobbled all my Cultural momentos. Being of the tippy one hundred Sites was assumed to be a thing of an honor, for every site had matched space, matched accessibility, and matched advertising, and therefore the only course to pop-fame was through word of yapper. Hai, the news of hundredthness forged a flabbergast gasp, but I stored the info at the aft of my thinker as mucho achievable. My familia never mentioned the Site—they probably didn't even know its pop-fame—until that day my mother, with dazzled peepers, enlightened me about a visitor waiting. So to the living room I trekked and found a woman kneeling on the center mat. She, who I knew to be Ambrosia, probably the tippiest adored person on the tele, tickled at me with the biggyest peepers on the Flapjack. Every year, they appeared to grow larger and larger, and many assumed she accomplished this with surgical tinkerings, but others asserted that they grew by their own accords. Every phenomena about her—her clothes, the way her pupils danced, her trembles—spoke the same words: "I need you."

Across from her, I sat, a mighty distance away.

My father trotted forward and said to her, "Mayhaps you would like some tea?" and he reached for a cup.

To this, my mother coughed in the archway, and my father stumbled backward as if he'd been shoved.

"I would mightily enjoy some tea," Ambrosia said, then peeked at me for a momento. "Mayhaps Newton-san would do me the honor?"

"Hai," said I, and repositioned to her side, while my mother yanked my father to the archway with her glare.

The cup to her yapper, she appeared to have only the strength to part her lips a slit. I tilted the cup and she sipped. This was the official fantasy of many Flapjack men, as polls identified, but the momento to me felt not so much like a dreambubble, but what I imagined a twisting stab in the gut to feel like.

"You're probably wondering what I'm doing here, true enough?" she said.

"Verily so," trembled I.

"Your Site brings me to you. Or pulls me, rather. Like a black hole." Her words flowed from her in gentle gusts. "I'm sure you know it has reached the tippy hundred. It's only a matter of tiempo before it reaches the tippy ten. By then you'll have actresses all over you."

"It's nice of you to say," said I. "But verily it's not my future you speak."

"Oh, but it is. I have a seventh sense for these things. The cause of my present pop-fame is that very sense. I seek out the rising treasures before their sparkle shines for all to see. This all means, of course, I'd like to take your stories to the tele. I'd like to play Humpty. Such a funny character, she is, and yet so tragic. It's the role I've been looking for. Dreaming of."

"It's…the tippiest honor for you to give me such praise—" I could hardly believe myself to be saying this, but it came out without a hindrance. "—however, Humpty is a woman with all her parts. You are not."

Her peepers thinned like a curtaining stage. "That I am well aware. My voids can be hidden."

"From the tele-eye, hai, but not from the thinkers of the spectators. They know of your missing parts. Your ghosts of female beauty will not be forgotten. Anyway, Humpty's parts must be seen. That is who she is."

"Newton-san." She nuzzled her stump against my hand. "Your Site has been a mighty source of pleasure to me since I discovered it. This pleasure I've shared with mucho influential and powerful people. Surely you won't forget all I've done for you."

"Forget, I will not. And though it pains me to speak the words, they are the words. A woman with missing parts cannot play Humpty." I lowered my peepers. "Gomen."

"Iie." She stood and grew taller than me. "The sorry one is I for you. Mucho days and years you'll spend regretting those words to me. A missed opportunity rots the thinker like fruit in the sun. Time only brings bitterness and worms."

After she whooshed out the archway, my parents took her place at my side.

"Newton-san," my father said. "Is your thinker aware of who that was?"

"Hai," said I.

"You could have found an actress to court," my mother said.

"Hai," said I.

They continued on and on and on, and I hai-ed and hai-ed and hai-ed, but what my thinker really boomed was iie, iie, iie. A fruit will rot verily, my thinker spat within, but through that bitter, stinky, buggy ugliness a seed is borne. And no matter how many fruits my familia or Ambrosia or anyone else sliced with their cutters, the trees would always keep growing eternal in that Magic Green Forest where Humpty lived, throwing parsnips at even the biggyest, loveliest Red eyes.

"The power of you," Humpty the Captivated Captivitized said, more real-appearing than I'd ever seen him. You see, most of the tiempo, the white-tuniced Wee-the-People fused into the pallor of the prison walls and floors, with their exposed skin tucked together in balls of sunken faces and conjoined feelers. Fact, the first tiempo trekking the halls, peepers blurry from tearbursts, I viewed mere invisible no-ones, whose existence only solidified in vinegar prayers. But now Humpty stood as a man of lines, sharpened and glowing with a beyond-the-barrera expression of self. "The power of you to protect Humpty is verily mighty."

"She is my amicus eternal," said I.

"But this power traverses the border of your strength for self. That I do not understand."

"Unimportant."

"Unimportant, you say? My thinker supposed all brainchildren should be cared for, not exposed upon a hill to wither away amongst the elemental virulence."

"My advice signifies not abortion but contortion. Ask not from where the power came from for me to protect my amicus, but rather: would I, Humpty, like to feel that power my own self? And if so, how?"

He sighed. "Such spoken shackles you burden me with."

"Mightier than the cage circum?"

"In a way."

"Then mayhaps it is tiempo to question the relevance of these walls."

"Relevance? Is not existence relevance enough?"

"You tell me."

"Iie." He sat again. "This is your story and not my place to speak of unknowns. So continue with your chatter-chains and bind me to your words. But if I suffocate, I will curse you in death."

"Fair enough."

As Ambrosia foretold, my Site did cultivate in pop-fame to the tippy ten. But actresses did not swarm the household. I assumed Ambrosia had alerted her colleagues that I would not consent to a partless woman, which intimated, in fact, every.

Days after my tippy tenness, a male visitor awaited me. He happy-faced when I passed through the arch, in a way like we were old amici. At the tiempo, my thinker played with the idea that mayhaps we had known one another at the gymnasium. His form I felt I recognized, or should recognize, but was unable to with the tiempo allotted—being the walk over.

"Salu, Newton-san," he said.

"Salu," said I.

"Mayhaps you recognize me."

The truth bit my neck. "Oh, hai!" I spoke louder than I wished, but attempted to suppress my embarrassment. "You're on the soap opera. One my mother watches day to day. You're a new character, true enough?"

"Hai, that I am. You're probably wondering what I'm doing here."

"Something to do with my Site?" said I.

"Verily so." He sipped his tea. "It's a terrible thing what Ambrosia has done to you. Terrible."

"And what thing is this?"

"Blacklisted, she's made you. To join with you now is married to crossing Ambrosia. Most telepersonalities fear getting prox to you."

"But not you, I see?"

"Oh, fear surges through my veins. Not due to our proxness, but the proposition I've yet to release."

"Proposition?"

"Hai. I..." By then, I noticed his body moved eternal. He tinkered, or tapped, or twiddled, or twitched at every momento, like a tree haunted by an incessant breeze. "I would like to take you to the tele myself. I, my own self, would play Humpty."

Shock! This I did not expect, and surely I thought my face reflected it. So I looked down, rearranged my features, and looked up once more. "You realize...you'd have to play a woman."

He nodded. "Hai, but I see no other way, if your Humpty is to keep her parts. These parts are important to you, I deduce, judging by Ambrosia's fury."

"Hai."

"Of course the spectators will always know she's being played by a man, but I'm not a well-known personality. Most televiewers have never even looked upon me. So that should aid imaginations in their thinkers' creation of Humpty, true enough?"

"That it would. But would the tele verily show my stories?"

"Fact. I've personally heard mighty a few directors expressing a desire to bring them to life. They simply have been unable to find the means. Means I am, or could be, with your sanctioned nod. So what say you, Newton-san? Shall Humpty meta to flesh and blood or remain silenced in the realm of shadowscript?"

"Hitherto, I would have interrupted you this momento and demanded an answer to that question," Humpty the Prisoner said, in a proud sort of manner.

"But you interrupt me with a statement in the stead?" said I. "This you consider an improvement?"

"I simply wished to inform you of my progress."

"And what exactly is this progression you speak of?"

"I...know not."

"You vowed to speak nada of unknowns, did you not?"

"I told you I would not, but vowed nada."

"And what's the difference between speaking and vowing?"

"Vowing lives in fragility, my thinker imagines. Promises can shatter, where speaking cannot. What you say is what you say, endpoint. I shall pledge nada."

"Nada at all?"

"Well...except to harken in return after my own words are released."

"And I vow the same. So with these promises, we are bound, true enough?"

"Verily so."

"I suppose we now live in fragility then, if what you said is correct. And I also must suppose your life of old was mucho mightier, when you pleaded to faceless forms in void-of-vow solitude."

"You...suppose in the wrong. If you were to disappear, more fragile then than now, I would feel."

"Then I shall continue with the story, and mayhaps I will not fade away."

"What say you?" said the Director to me. "Which one do you prefer?"

For the past mucho horas, the Director, the new Humpty, and I had harkened to could-be Newton after Newton after Newton. And of them, I said, "None."

"None?" the Director said.

"Hai. They...they speak the lines as if the lines are tippy important. They speak nothing of the unspoken."

"Your meaning escapes me."

"Newton-san," Humpty said, on the other side of me. "If you wish to play Newton your own self, you can marry in contract your body to the story. Then the only way the creators can bring the tale to the tele is if you are Newton."

"It...is so," the Director said and coughed. "Such things have occurred in the past, but more often than less, such an attachment entails a clear path to cancellation."

"Fear not, Director," said I. "I will not force my own self upon you, as many men would. But I do ask for the opportunity to audition. The choice then will be verily your own. You may have the tale of Newton and Humpty whether you choose me or do not."

"So be it," the Director said, like a burped baby.

To the center mat, I stood with Humpty. And let me say that though this was an audition for the tele, it meant to me tippy more. This was a test of sorts, and I forgot the Director even existed. I found myself floating in a dreambubble once again. A group of young men passed by, and did the expected.

"Does it ever bother you?" said I.

"What?" Humpty said.

"Their pointing and laughing. They speak such terrible things."

"What is so terrible about what they say? Tell me their words."

"I cannot."

"You can. You're simply a Hopper Lite who fears even inflicting welcomed rudeness."

"You want me to say it? Very well. They call you mannish."

"I care not."

"They think you are the ugliest woman on the Flapjack."

"Hai, but do you?"

Nada, said I. Nada, nada, and more nada, for that was all I could say. A nada formed from words never spoken to my familia; from the muffled screams of the Green butterflies I chopped; from my own imprisoned tears. A nada that replaced the waterfall of the broken fountain maiden. And a nada especially made of Humpty's ugliness. For even if the whole of Flapjack proclaimed Humpty the ugliest woman of all, I knew I had the power to drown out all their voices, if I allowed myself to open up and set free the hidden words. But nada, said I, and the words remained hidden. But I heard them, inside, loud as a lie.

"My thinker resolves to interrupt you with a question this tiempo," said I.

Humpty trembled as one who had seen a spirit, or realized he was one. "I would rather you continued with the story."

"And had I not rathered the same thing every tiempo you interrupted me, I might honor your request. So here's the question: did I get the part or didn't I?"

For a mighty tiempo, he stared forward, frail. Then he grew mighty once more. "Whether you did get the part or not, I know not, but that is not the real question to be asked."

"Which is?"

"Did you or did you not pass the test? Your own test."

"And did I?"

"Your peepers say hai."

"As speak your own."

The Tele Adventures of Newton and Humpty was no difficult over-and-undertaking, but there existed no mightier gift than feigning such. Pop-fame blessed me like a magic stone, illuminating everyever my familia's peepers became prox, and spat out a sparkly ray with hypnotic powers. "Newton the Telepersonality is too busy for familia business," said the stone, in their thinkers. "Leave the boy be, you smally somebody." And chopped I no more women and touched no more cutters. I did, however, play-chop women-shaped comper forms, and touched improper cuttery props. And so the Redness of my life meta-ed into a reddish hue which could be peeped by fans (including my familia) wearing thornless rose-colored spectator-spectacles.

Mucho tiempo I spent at Humpty's home for the practice of lines, or at least such was the (mayhaps unneeded) justification. He was my amicus after all.

"What is it about these stories of mine?" said I, to him and my own self. "Why rise when others fall?"

"Humpty is a woman who lacks the lacks of womanhood," he said.

"She hasn't the common personality of anyone you'll meet eternal."

"And yet those who gaze her with fervent peepers dub her ugly. Who would care for ugliness so mightily?"

"And who would so mightily create such ugliness?"

I preferred not to lie to him, so silence swallowed us.

Finally, "Does it feels strange?" said I.

"What?" he said.

"Wearing pink for the tele."

He sipped tea with more-than-usual shaky feelers. "I don't focus on my own self. Such an activity would beget too many unanswerable questions."

"Such as?"

"What does it mean to be a man wearing pink? How can an unadorned man once called handsome be then made a treasured but horrid woman?"

A dreambubble I knew this was not. The real Humpty hacked on such self-spawned question marks until answers vomited forth, no matter how bitter the bile.

The question of Humpty's popularity did not release her stranglehold. There was mas to her attractive unattractiveness than simple rarity. I began to wonder—

"I know the end already," Humpty the White said.

"The end?" said I.

"The answer to that question of questions."

"Release your thinker then, amicus."

Humpty stretched his legs out on the prison floor, as if preparing for a dash. "Humpty intrigues the thinker due to the questions she spawns. Not the questions she asks, but the questions of we. Why do I live in a cage and not in a tree? Why does Humpty feel laetitia with her parts intact? Why do you think she's beautiful?"

"True enough, you capture the end, and your words have shattered this story like a parsnip through a window. I can no longer tell it."

Humpty's face tightened. "Forgive my insolence! A word and I'll smash my head upon the wall to dislodge this parasite!"

"Hold. That specific story was rather boring anyway, with all the self-analysis and hubbub. It's better obliterated, so that we may continue to a mightier image."

I helloed and entered Humpty's quarters, to find him in his beddy bye, dressed in his pink tele-tunic. The desire to run twirled me, but my hello must have flicked his thinker, for I heard him stir.

"Newton, I..." he said.

My yapper exported nada.

"I wear it sometimes," he said. "It...aids in getting into character."

"Of course," said I. "Shall we practice the lines anon?"

"Hai."

We stood prox and spoke the words.

I realized (or mayhaps could no longer deny to my own self) that neither of us acted a whittle whit. The acting took place outside of our tele life, when we read not the lines. His want was to wear a pink tunic. His want was to be a woman. He was Humpty, but had to pretend to be someone else. Because Flapjack demanded the lie. And on that day, I acquired my first real enemy.

Humpty the White stared at Wall #4 for mucho heartbeats. Then, "Wee-the-People have always venerated the Flapjack for its freedom. But who is the freer? At least my own people can be who we think we are."

I happy-faced. "Brainchildren grow up so fast, do they not?"

"Verily so. And did you go to war against the Flapjack? Is this what brought you to me?"

"Hai and hai. But I fear your thinker has been misled by my terminology. My battles involved no blood, no Red, no cutters."

"Good. I have no taste for such matters."

"You lie like a child, but I appreciate the intention. If only I could bestow upon you a mightier adventure than what occurred, but it was a tippy snoozy process of sitting at the comper, searching, searching, searching. Years I spent trying to understand my enemy. The mightiest shock burst from the fact that the answers were all out there, broken apart, as shame-sham shards. Piece them together was the only task, and not a difficult one. I own not an extraordinary thinker. Anyone could have learned what I learned. The vomity truth is that no one wished to see past the walls of their cage. The question now is: do you wish to see? Do you desire the truth of Flapjack?"

"I...do. However, I would appreciate if you would speak not the truth to me direct. Place it in a dreambubble, if you could."

"I can."

To understand the Flapjack, said I to Humpty, I required answers. And so I gathered ingredients from all over the Flapjack to summon a mighty wizard. At last the day came when I mixed everything together in a biggy black cauldron in the most mysterious section of Magic Green Forest, at the spot of Humpty's nestplace.

The cauldron erupted with fire, then the Wizard whooshed, adorned with a tunic of Red. "You shake me from a biggy slumber, smally boy," he said. "This had better be tippy important."

"I wish to know about the Flapjack," said I.

His laughter boomed, and the leaves vibrated circum. "You summon me for a knowledge that will bring you only mightier gray-thoughts?"

"My outcomings are not your concern."

"Verily so. What you wish, I will give you."

So we both sat on leafy mounds, though in truth he hovered a bugspace above.

"Of the history of Flapjack, what do you grasp?" he said.

"Not mucho," said I. "My people lived once as groundlings, but crafted the Flapjack and rose above."

"And do you know the reason for this crafty crafting?"

"The progression of technology, I assume."

He laughed loud, but not leaf-shaking. "Twas the progression of understanding which birthed the Flapjack. You see, smally one, mucho tiempo in the before, civilization grew to be mightily conscious of the causes of human behavior. Every action of every human spoke of their genetics, their environment, their past. Many humans expected a more enlightened society to be borne with such knowledge. Verily, humans were tippy capable of living lives of laetitia and balanced authority. But occurred, this did not. The civilization of old fought back like an angered trollbeast. Ideological strangleholds squeezed tighter with this war for and against modifications. The Flapjack was created by the Merican sect that fought the hardest against the Enlightenment of Understanding."

"Is Merica not a mythological place?"

"Twas real. This Merican sect hugged an ideology which justified the taking of resources from all over the planet. But this sect realized that ideologies could not last eternal. So they replaced their ideology with an automated resource abductor. The Flapjack, this is. Your culture has meta-ed much over time, in texture, however one thing holds eternal. Your machines abduct resources from the humans on the surface, killing more than many. You use mas energy than all the groundlings in combination, and you are one percent of the population. That is your truth."

"I will have to burst the dreambubble if I'm to continue," said I.

"Continue," Humpty said.

The knowledge I had acquired bansheed to flee, and so for the next teleshow, spoke I not the lines Flapjack expected, but the lines of my real self.

"Something blazes within, Humpty," said I. "A force wishing to be freed."

"What?" Humpty said.

I held her shoulders. "You're the most beautiful woman I've ever known. I love you." I kissed her.

Humpty's jitters meta-ed to fleshquakes, and he stumbled back.

Faced I to the tele-eye. "The things done and the things not done, this is our choice. We must meta the ways that pop the dreambubbles of our whispery hopes. We must meta that which spreads suffering to those below. We know our energy spawns from the ground, but do we ponder the how to the Flapjack's forever-flap? We fire no weapons. We press no buttons. Direct, we do nada to the groundlings, but can disconnectedness illusionate as a comfy-warm void of responsibility? Iie. The mechanical feelers that ravage the lands below animate these lives of ours. Let these feelers serve as metal ghosts of murdered history, so that we may harken the need to fall to grace once more."

I turned to Humpty.

But only a handsome man stared in reply.

"The worst part was not that a machine took me from my familia to this prison," said I. "The worst was that my words meant nada to them, unquestionable."

"But Humpty harkened your words. Mayhaps he will—"

"Mayhaps nothing. He was not the real Humpty. The words will not meta him."

"But they have meta-ed me!"

I happy-faced. "Verily so, and I finally understand how and why. The Wizard could not explain to me why this prison exists, but you have enlightened me."

"How could I enlighten you before my own self?"

"These things happen." I pressed my feelers against Wall #4 and its imperfection. "This prison hangs below the Flapjack like a cancer. A great population lives in this prison, and are born in this prison, and expire in this prison. You and your people are here because your genetics dub you mas viable to destroy the Flapjack's automated consumption. The ideological forces of this space force those tendencies to dormancy, and keep you all subdued. Viz, the Flapjack wins. Those who would fight are stuck here. There's no hope. I fear that's the end of the story."

"Iie!" He stood. "As I still live and breathe, your amicus eternal I will be. And together, we will smash this chumming place until the Flapjack falls to the forests, where we may live among the trees once more!"

"Now that sounds like the real Humpty."

"Humpty, I am."

ABOUT THE AUTHOR

Jeremy C. Shipp is an author whose written creations inhabit various magazines, anthologies, and drawers. These include over 40 publications, the likes of *Cemetery Dance, ChiZine,* and *The Bizarro Starter Kit (blue).* While preparing for the forthcoming collapse of civilization, Jeremy enjoys living in Southern California in a moderately haunted Victorian farmhouse with his wife, Lisa, and their legion of yard gnomes. He's currently working on many stories and novels and is losing his hair, though not because of the ghosts. This is his first published collection, and his debut novel is called *Vacation.* Feel free to visit his online home at www.jeremycshipp.com, but beware the robotic parsnips and rabid coconut monkeys.